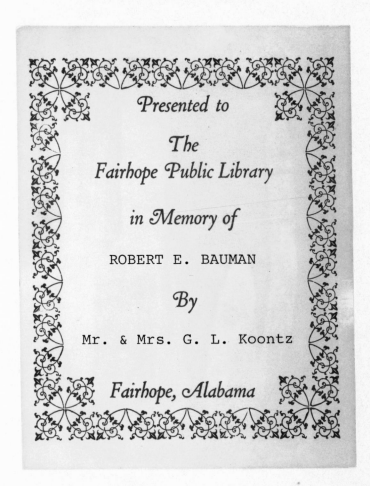

Aunt Agatha Plays
Tournament Bridge

FREDDIE NORTH

85-553

faber and faber
LONDON · BOSTON

First published in 1984
by Faber and Faber Limited
3 Queen Square, London WC1N 3AU
Filmset by Wilmaset, Birkenhead
Printed in Great Britain by
Whitstable Litho Limited,
Whitstable, Kent

British Library Cataloguing in Publication Data

North, Freddie
Aunt Agatha plays tournament bridge
1. Contract bridge
I. Title
795.41′53   GV1282.3

ISBN 0-571-13341-X
ISBN 0-571-13342-8 Pbk

My capacity for astonishment is only exceeded by my ability to suffer partner's idiocies with relative good grace.

Aunt Agatha's self-portrait—
though many would disagree
with the last part!

Contents

Acknowledgements

I am indebted to *Bridge Magazine* for permission to include some material which has appeared in that excellent publication.

My thanks are also due to Gus Calderwood for his diligence in endeavouring to eradicate my analytical errors.

Foreword

You would think in over thirty years of teaching, often at the very lowest level, and even longer playing, often at the very highest level, that I would have come across just about every type of person imaginable. Good, bad and indifferent. Effusive, voluble and extrovert. Shy, reticent and introvert. You name them, I've met them, and in most cases could categorize them. But there is one notable exception: Freddie's Aunt Agatha. She is an extraordinary woman who virtually defies classification.

When I first met Aunt Agatha, I couldn't help thinking that perhaps it was lucky she wasn't born in the seventeenth century. In those days I am sure she would have been accused of being a witch, and terrible things happened to the unfortunates who were found guilty of witchcraft. Legend has it that in order to prove their innocence or guilt their thumbs were tied to their opposite toes and they were flung into the nearest river. If they floated, they were guilty. If they sank, innocent. But I digress. Aunt Agatha is a twentieth-century living legend, and I shall never forget our first encounter. When I congratulated her on a well-played hand she replied, 'Whatever women do they must perform twice as well as men to be thought half as good. Luckily this is not difficult' (a remark credited originally to Charlotte Whitton, Mayor of Ottawa).

There is no doubt that Aunt Agatha is a really tough competitor whose looks belie her ability. On the surface there may appear to be an aura of cherubic innocence and gentleness, but under that misleading exterior exists a clear mind, an aggressive nature and an almost paranoiac desire to win. Often brilliant, invariably bellicose and always dangerous, Aunt Agatha sets the scene for many a fascinating hand. In this book, Freddie seems to have captured much of the atmosphere of the battlefield, so that reading and learning will be a dual pleasure for the reader.

The only request I would make of Freddie's aunt is this: 'Please keep off my patch.'

NICO GARDENER

Introduction
The Chief Characters

Such is the charisma of Aunt Agatha that one might almost be forgiven for omitting details of the dramatis personae and concentrating solely on the star of the show. But bridge is a game for four people, and while Aunt Agatha may dismiss the others as insignificant appendages there would be no story without them. The props, the costumes, the make-up, the chorus—they are indispensable to the top of the bill, and so it is that players like Mildred, Sally and Issie so frequently set the scene which allows Aunt Agatha to bask in the spotlight.

Aunt Agatha likes winning and positively hates losing. She doesn't suffer fools gladly and is inclined to vent her feelings without pulling her punches, often to the acute embarrassment of everyone present. On the credit side, she is virtually capable of winning matches almost entirely under her own steam. She lives quietly in the country, in a lovely old pseudo-Tudor cottage where tranquility and serenity herald the approach to a picturesque garden, so rich in scent and colour, and on to the waterfall at the end of the pergola. Such a peaceful scene gives no inkling of the tigerish qualities that quickly manifest themselves in my aunt the moment she sits at the bridge table. Indeed, it is often enough just for bridge to be mentioned for an immediate metamorphosis to take place. The somewhat frail, kindly old lady is hardly recognizable as Mrs Jekyll becomes Mrs Hyde, and bonhomie is replaced by aggression. These tiger-like qualities make her a tremendous battler who doesn't know the meaning of the word defeat, and doesn't want to, but she is not the easiest person in the world to partner. Volunteers are scarce, and those that can be browbeaten into the role are equally inconspicuous, which brings us to Mildred:

Mildred lives in a block of flats only three miles away from Aunt Agatha. A mousy, nervous woman, she is afraid of everything, including her own shadow, but especially of Aunt Agatha. Perhaps that is why she so often partners my aunt. The royal decree is issued and Mildred is too frightened to invent pressing engagements elsewhere. She is a fairly solid but unimaginative player. Often her bids emerge with about as much conviction as one would expect of President Reagan praising the KGB. Apart from her timidity, perhaps her worse fault is her penchant for playing parrot bridge, relying on clichés and slogans rather than thinking for herself. Having said that, she often makes the winning bid after one of her soul-searching trances, and if the opposition are foolish enough to be lulled into a false sense of optimism, that's too bad. Mildred is as honest as the day is long, and those who know her well would doubtless label her totally predictable. Mildred's neighbour is Sally:

Sally is a reasonable player whom one would hardly notice unless someone pointed her out to you. Undemonstrative and quiet by nature, she performs her function of making up the numbers with admirable consistency and lack of fuss. No doubt because of her introverted and unassuming personality she rarely hits the headlines—remarks that certainly do *not* apply to one of her regular partners:

Professor Issie Rabinovinski. Issie is a volatile, impish extrovert who has never quite grown up. Although a Professor of Psychology, he revels in his fourth-form humour and takes a special delight in *trying* to get the better of Aunt Agatha—not an easy task. Once asked to define bad luck he replied, 'It's like this. A chap wins half a girl in a raffle—and then finds he's got the half that talks. That's real bad luck.' Issie is a fair player of the cards and is a bold and carefree bidder who, like so many of his type, probably enjoys more success than his skill merits. Issie's background is something of a mystery. Superficially he seems to do nothing, but he spends a lot of time away from his bachelor apartment, only a few miles from Aunt Agatha's cottage but in the opposite direction to Mildred and Sally, and these trips are never accounted for with any degree of conviction. Rumour has it that he is engaged in secret work for the Home Office, but if this is so he gives not the slightest indication of it. I find it hard to believe that anyone so flippant and light-hearted is involved in murky and secret deeds, but there is no doubt that Issie is an interesting enigma.

1

Almost Double Dummy

Perhaps one tends to think of Aunt Agatha chiefly as a rubber-bridge player, but in fact she is quite a dab hand at the board game. However, the trouble with competitive bridge is that you need a permanent partner, or at any rate a partner who is prepared to play long sessions with you. At rubber bridge Aunt Agatha can foist herself on others by cutting into their game, and there's not much anyone can do about it, but finding a regular partner . . . that's quite different. Masochists are not so liberally dispersed around the world.

Issie, who occasionally partners Aunt Agatha, was once asked why he didn't form a permanent partnership with her. In typical Issie style he replied, 'There's no harm in kissing the nun, you know. The trouble starts when you get into the habit!' Issie will never grow up, but he's no fool.

Unpredictable as always, Aunt Agatha is quite capable of achieving the impossible—that is the plus side for anyone crazy enough to consider partnering her. Watch my aunt in action on this hand from the 1980 Charity Challenge Cup. The hand was submitted by Mrs Rixi Markus, OBE, for many years the world's number one woman player.

E–W game   ♠ 3 2
Dealer East   ♡ A K Q 4
                  ◇ A K 7 5
                  ♣ A 7 6

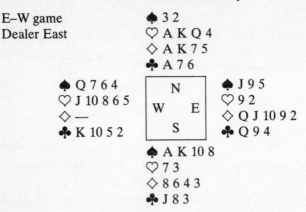

♠ Q 7 6 4   ♠ J 9 5
♡ J 10 8 6 5   ♡ 9 2
◇ —   ◇ Q J 10 9 2
♣ K 10 5 2   ♣ Q 9 4

                  ♠ A K 10 8
                  ♡ 7 3
                  ◇ 8 6 4 3
                  ♣ J 8 3

Aunt Agatha (North) plays in 3NT (1 ♡–1 ♠; 3NT) and East leads the queen of diamonds. West is put to an immediate discard and chooses a low club.

With only eight tricks on top, Rixi suggests, declarer will play a spade towards dummy, and when East plays low he will call for the eight. Now nothing can stop him coming to nine tricks. So the recommended defence is for East to hop up with the knave of spades on the first round, thus cutting the communications and thwarting declarer in his effort to make more than two spades.

'Against me,' declared Aunt Agatha proudly, 'they can play the knave of spades at any time they like—after the initial lead—but I shall always make my contract.'

Aunt Agatha's solution? She played a low club towards the dummy at trick two. Now try and stop her making nine tricks. This is how the play may develop:

1. If East goes up with the ♣ Q—North wins the diamond return (West discarding a spade) and plays a spade towards dummy. East contributes the knave and South wins with the ace. Now four rounds of hearts leave West to cash his fifth heart, but then he has to concede an additional trick in one of the black suits.

2. If East wins with the ♣ 9, dummy ducking—North takes the return as before and plays a spade to the knave and ace. Now a club is led from dummy. If West plays the ten, North plays the ace and proceeds as before. West will eventually have to concede an additional trick in spades. If West plays the ♣ K instead of the ten, he is allowed to hold the trick. Subsequently the ♣ A is cashed and West thrown on lead with the fourth heart to concede the additional trick in spades.

3. If East plays low on the first club—West wins with the ten. The heart return is won by North, and declarer plays as in 2 above.

4. If East plays low on the first club and West wins with the king and returns a spade—East is allowed to hold this trick. Subsequently the two top spades and three top hearts force a diamond discard. The ace and another diamond then leave East with no option but to play away from his ♣ Q 9.

Yes, one has to admit, Aunt Agatha is certainly unpredictable. Difficult contracts are usually made at the gallop. Impossible tasks take a shade longer. I shall come later to a painful memory of Aunt Agatha at large in a pairs contest. First, though, a few highlights from one of her 'at home' matches.

2

The Challenge Match

Aunt Agatha's 'at home' matches are usually memorable events. Things happen in that august household that you would hardly think possible—bridgewise, I mean. You think I exaggerate? Well, just wait and see.

Heaven help me when Aunt Agatha reads this book, but I have warned her that if I am to be involved with her little games then I cannot be completely silenced. Bridge players are entitled to know of the misdeeds of others, and although Aunt Agatha is an exception to virtually every rule I know and every law that was ever promulgated, she possesses no magic cloak of anonymity. Indeed, I believe if the truth were really known she is a fanatical subscriber to the philosophy of that famous actress who decreed, 'Speak well of me if you can, speak evil of me if you must, but for God's sake talk about me!'

Anyway, Aunt Agatha had challenged Issie to a 32-board match, and all those familiar with these two colourful characters would no doubt have predicted that the sparks would fly. One of the early hands, which would have done credit to any fifth of November evening, set the pattern.

Aunt Agatha was sitting West, vulnerable against non-vulnerable opponents, and this was her hand:

♠ K Q J 10 7
♥ K J 9
⋄ K J 10
♣ J 2

Annoyingly, South opened 3NT. What should Aunt Agatha bid? Deeply suspicious that she was being jockeyed out of something that was rightfully hers, she doubled. But even her stern and authoritative tone did not prevent North redoubling. Without any visible sign of distress Aunt Agatha passed and led the king of spades. This was the full deal:

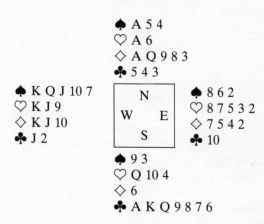

```
                ♠ A 5 4
                ♡ A 6
                ◇ A Q 9 8 3
                ♣ 5 4 3
♠ K Q J 10 7      N        ♠ 8 6 2
♡ K J 9                    ♡ 8 7 5 3 2
◇ K J 10      W     E      ◇ 7 5 4 2
♣ J 2            S         ♣ 10
                ♠ 9 3
                ♡ Q 10 4
                ◇ 6
                ♣ A K Q 9 8 7 6
```

Issie was at the wheel, and as he surveyed the dummy it was clear that he liked what he saw. Furthermore, he proceeded to make the most of it. After the ace of spades and six top clubs, this was the position:

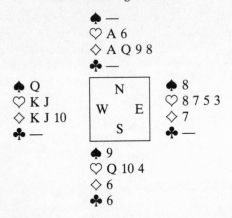

The six of clubs now completed a triple squeeze on Aunt Agatha. She did her best by throwing a diamond, but dummy parted with a heart and the rest of the tricks were won via the diamond finesse.

'Now, let's see,' said Issie, 'that's 3NT doubled and redoubled with four overtricks, plus 300 for game. No less than 1550, I think.'

Of course Aunt Agatha made an unfortunate decision when she stuck the redouble. To bid 4 ♠ or 4 ♡ would have been less costly, despite the vulnerability, but Aunt Agatha does not retreat too readily. I get the impression that she considers back-pedalling rather infra dig. Anyway, this board had been the first one played in the other room, where there had also been a dramatic result. It is pointless relating the actual bidding, because Aunt Agatha's other pair had a monumental muddle and none of their auction made sense. The trouble arose because South thought they were playing Precision, a system she and her partner had been discussing with a view to trying it out when next they played. North, on the other hand, was sure they were playing Acol—the Precision system being held over for a less momentous occasion. Not being quite certain whether the gambling 3NT was part of Precision, South settled for 2 ♣ (11–15 points and a good club suit) and North, with her giant opposite an 'Acol 2 ♣ bid', settled for 7NT, despite a show of teeth from West. East led a spade and, recovering from her shock when she saw the dummy, North duly emerged with all thirteen tricks in a similar manner to the learned Professor. Plus 1520 to Aunt Agatha's team left her just one imp down on the board!

THE LAST SAY

The redoubling area is one of those mysterious regions where neither light nor darkness ever reigns supreme; a grey area where only the closest-knit partnerships seem to have any idea of how the dice are loaded. In the above example, East's hands were tied and it was left to West to try and gauge the prospects. Obviously South had a solid club suit, and North must have at least two aces, so unless North–South were lying in their teeth, 3NT was going to zoom home. Furthermore, a third ace with North—likely enough on the bidding—was going to prove a real thorn in West's side. Taking all these factors into account, I believe West should have buried her pride and started a rescue operation: 4 ♠, or 4 ♣ followed by a redouble over the inevitable(?) double, has much to commend it and seems infinitely preferable to the ostrich-like pass.

Luck is supposed to level out over a sufficiently long period, and this was a classic example of 'bad luck minus good luck equals zero', or almost zero. Aunt Agatha was unlucky to be caught in such a fierce pincer grip in her room, but then the good fortune came bounding back when her other pair made a complete nonsense of their system only to surface smelling of roses.

There were some glorious opportunities missed on the next hand, but it must be admitted that Issie pulled off a rare coup against Aunt Agatha.

East–West game
Dealer West

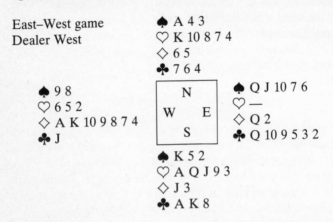

♠ A 4 3
♡ K 10 8 7 4
◇ 6 5
♣ 7 6 4

♠ 9 8
♡ 6 5 2
◇ A K 10 9 8 7 4
♣ J

♠ Q J 10 7 6
♡ —
◇ Q 2
♣ Q 10 9 5 3 2

♠ K 5 2
♡ A Q J 9 3
◇ J 3
♣ A K 8

The bidding in Room 1 was a little unusual in that West decided against starting with a pre-emptive bid in diamonds.

S	W	N	E
—	No	No	No
1 ♡	2◇	3♡	No
4 ♡	No	No	No

West began with two top diamonds and then switched to a trump. Subsequently declarer lost one club and one spade. So that was 50 points to Issie's team.

In Room 2, where Aunt Agatha was West and Issie South, the contract was also 4 ♡ but, predictably, Aunt Agatha had started the ball rolling with a pre-emptive bid of 3 ◇.

Aunt Agatha also cashed her top diamonds but then switched to the nine of spades. Dummy won and led the seven of hearts to declarer's knave and West's two, East discarding a club. The ace of hearts followed, dummy being careful to play the eight while East discarded a spade. Having cunningly preserved the three and four of hearts Issie now cashed the ace of clubs. Noting the fall of the knave he deliberated for fully two minutes. Should he cash a second spade or a second club? Only one of Aunt Agatha's cards remained a secret—but what a secret! Eventually the king of spades emerged, and when Aunt Agatha followed suit one could almost sense Issie's heart doing double somersaults. This was the position:

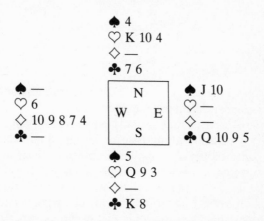

The three of hearts, and four from dummy, ensured that Aunt Agatha won this trick—her third. But now the enforced ruff and discard enabled Issie to win in hand and discard a club from dummy. The queen of hearts was then overtaken with the king to produce the following three-card ending:

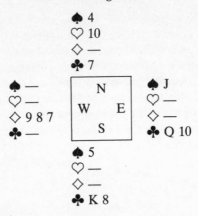

The ten of hearts squeezed East into submission, and a gleeful Issie started entering up the score.

Aunt Agatha knew that she had been caught napping and was livid with herself for letting Issie set her up. She recalled that she had once pulled off a similar coup against Issie at rubber bridge, but that seemed poor consolation now.* Besides, Issie was becoming unbearable, with his sly winks at his partner and repeated mutterings about two for one being good value.

The funny thing was that only two of the players, Issie and Aunt Agatha, really knew what had happened. The others were still mystified by it all even when the match was over. It just hadn't made sense, but further discussion on the subject was quickly vetoed by Aunt Agatha as she glared at everyone in turn.

---

*page 60, *Bridge with Aunt Agatha*.

THE LAST SAY

Opportunities for this sort of coup—losing an unnecessary trump trick in order to regain it via a ruff and discard which then sets up a squeeze—are comparatively rare but highly satisfying when they occur. Full marks to Issie for recognizing the situation and carefully preserving his small trumps, although of course Aunt Agatha should have been alerted to the impending danger.

Perhaps one should say this. Whenever you hold two or three small trumps and there is a danger that you might be thrown in to concede a profitable trick for declarer, consider unblocking at once. And if the declarer seems to be going to great lengths to preserve a trump smaller than yours—perhaps you should unblock automatically.

Although there was no swing on the next hand, I thought Aunt Agatha deserved a bonus award for technique.

Love all
Dealer West

     ♠ A J 5
     ♡ K Q 5
     ◇ A Q 6
     ♣ A 5 4 3

```
        N
    W       E
        S
```

     ♠ K 9 7 4 3
     ♡ A J 4
     ◇ K 7 4
     ♣ Q J

Both teams reached 6 ♠ by South, and received the lead of the ten of hearts. How should declarer plan the play?

This was the full deal:

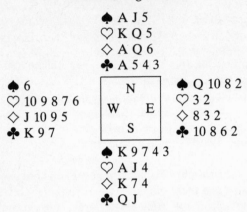

Issie's player won the heart lead in hand and immediately led a low spade to the knave and queen. Subsequently she was able to pick up the remainder of the spades and the king of clubs to land her contract.

Aunt Agatha, now sitting South, also won the heart lead in her hand but, instead of tackling spades at once, took the club finesse. When this was successful she embarked on a safety play in trumps. The ace first and then, having returned to hand, she played low towards the knave. Twelve tricks made.

Unlucky to find there was no swing, Aunt Agatha, because your handling of this situation deserved a better reward. I would love to have cheated and given East the singleton queen of spades. That would have been real justice. But my professional pride as a reporter of the facts just doesn't permit such flights of fancy.

THE LAST SAY

Although one declarer's carelessness was not punished on this occasion, there was a lesson to be learnt: get your priorities in order. There are two important issues at stake: (*a*) the position of the king of clubs, and (*b*) the division of the trump suit. One cannot do much about (*a*)—the finesse is either right or wrong. But the handling of the trump suit is quite a different matter. One can play for the jackpot—to win all five tricks—or one can take a safety play which will guard against a blank queen with East. Clearly one cannot determine how to handle (*b*) until one knows the result of (*a*). So declarer should take the club finesse before playing trumps.

The next hand again features Aunt Agatha in a role that could well be entitled 'I did it my way'.

East–West game
Dealer West

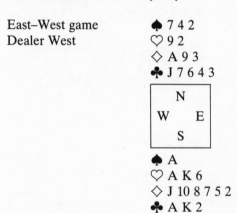

♠ 7 4 2
♡ 9 2
♢ A 9 3
♣ J 7 6 4 3

♠ A
♡ A K 6
♢ J 10 8 7 5 2
♣ A K 2

Issie's team played in the indifferent contract of 3NT, going one down after an initial spade lead. In Aunt Agatha's room, where she was South, this was the bidding:

S	W	N	E
—	No	No	No
1 ♢	No	2 ♢	Dble
5 ♢	Dble	No	No
No			

The six of spades was led. How should South play?

I suppose that ordinary mortals, like you and me, would play West for the missing diamond honours. If he split, we would then take a heart ruff and concede one diamond and one club. If he refused to split his honours on the first two rounds, we would leave the bare ace of diamonds in dummy and turn our attention to clubs. If the queen of clubs won the third round we could then dispose of our losing heart on a good club. West would ruff, but that would be his second and last trick. Time to look at the full hand and see how we would have got on:

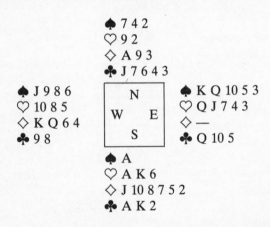

```
                    ♠ 7 4 2
                    ♡ 9 2
                    ◇ A 9 3
                    ♣ J 7 6 4 3
   ♠ J 9 8 6           N           ♠ K Q 10 5 3
   ♡ 10 8 5                         ♡ Q J 7 4 3
   ◇ K Q 6 4      W        E        ◇ —
   ♣ 9 8              S            ♣ Q 10 5
                    ♠ A
                    ♡ A K 6
                    ◇ J 10 8 7 5 2
                    ♣ A K 2
```

Yes, our plan would have been all right, but nothing like elegant enough for Aunt Agatha. At trick two she led a low diamond, and when West played small she called for the nine. A spade ruff, followed by the ace and king of hearts, a heart ruff, a second spade ruff and then three rounds of clubs reduced the hand to this position, with East to lead:

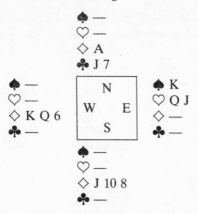

East consulted the ceiling (it is amazing how many bridge players look for divine inspiration from the ceiling—Aunt Agatha calls it the Belshazzar syndrome) and wriggled unhappily on her chair. Eventually she played a heart, not that it mattered. West's second 'sure' trump trick disappeared into thin air in as neat a smother play as you could ever hope to see.

'You know,' confided my aunt to me later on, 'I always thought smother plays only happened in books. This is the first time I have executed one in real life.'

What could I say but, 'Yes, Aunt Agatha, you certainly engineered it beautifully.'

THE LAST SAY

Note Aunt Agatha's technique once she had embarked on a smother play. It was necessary to reduce her trumps to the same number as West's while at the same time eliminating her side suits. When East was thrown in at trick ten it was essential that she could not play a suit held by the declaring side.

The next hand illustrated a slight variation in technique, but it made an enormous difference.

Game all
Dealer North

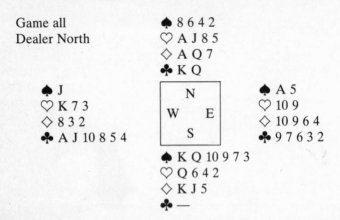

Both teams bid to 6 ♠ and both Wests led the ace of clubs.

In the first room Issie was South, the declarer. He ruffed the ace of clubs, led a diamond to dummy and played a spade which East ducked. Issie won with the queen of spades and played a diamond back to dummy. He then cashed the king of clubs—on which he discarded a heart—and the king of diamonds before exiting with a low spade to East's ace. East could do no better than get off lead with the ten of hearts, South and West playing low and dummy's knave winning the trick. Issie returned to hand with a trump and then fingered the queen and six of hearts in turn. Eventually the six of hearts was favoured—and so were the opponents, to the tune of 100 points.

In the other room Aunt Agatha was South. Ruffing the club in her hand she also entered dummy with a diamond and led a spade. Again East ducked and Aunt Agatha won with the queen. But now she led a heart to dummy, calling for the knave when West played low. She continued with the king of clubs, throwing a heart from her hand, the king of diamonds, the ace of hearts and then a spade to East's ace. Poor East was now helpless. She had to concec̓ ⸱ ⸱ ⸱ff and discard, and that was Aunt Agatha's twelfth trick.

THE LAST SAY

Issie's timing was less than perfect, while Aunt Agatha's was spot on. I recall that Issie was most reluctant to admit that he had made a mistake as he kept on repeating, 'Complete guess on the hearts. A complete guess.' But the beauty of Aunt Agatha's play is that once the king of hearts is located with West, it doesn't matter whether East holds one, two or three hearts. She succeeds anyway.

Although both Easts ducked the first round of spades without the flicker of an eyelid their technique must be open to question. The danger of being thrown in at a less propitious moment is a live one, so, at the small risk of crashing partner's possible trump honour, there is a lot to be said for going in with the ace immediately. If East does this and then exits safely with, say, a trump, an interesting point emerges with regard to the play of the heart suit. On the first round, when the knave holds, East will, perforce, have to play the ten or the nine. Now, you may say that either of these cards will alert South into playing the queen the next time around and not a low one. Maybe, but East should also play the nine or ten from a holding of 10 9 x with the express hope of misleading the declarer when he has to make the critical decision on the next round. So be warned!

On the next hand of interest Mildred (North) played in the safe contract of 5 ♣, making six, while Issie and his partner were a little wide of the mark when they pressed on to 6NT.

Game all
Dealer North

♠ 9 7 2
♡ 6
♢ A J 9
♣ A K J 5 3 2

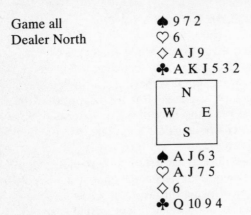

♠ A J 6 3
♡ A J 7 5
♢ 6
♣ Q 10 9 4

This was the bidding in Issie's room:

S (Issie)	W	N	E
—	—	1 ♣	1 ♡
1 ♠	No	3 ♣	No
3 ♡	No	3 ♠	No
4NT	No	5 ♡	No
6NT	No	No	No

Against this strange-looking contract West led the king of hearts and Issie was faced with the problem of having to find three extra tricks. He had a small measure of success when he ducked the opening lead and West continued with the queen of hearts. What plans would you make to give yourself the best chance of success?

This was the full hand:

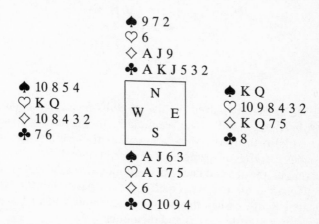

```
                    ♠ 9 7 2
                    ♡ 6
                    ◇ A J 9
                    ♣ A K J 5 3 2
    ♠ 10 8 5 4         N          ♠ K Q
    ♡ K Q                         ♡ 10 9 8 4 3 2
    ◇ 10 8 4 3 2    W     E       ◇ K Q 7 5
    ♣ 7 6              S          ♣ 8
                    ♠ A J 6 3
                    ♡ A J 7 5
                    ◇ 6
                    ♣ Q 10 9 4
```

Issie won the queen of hearts with his ace, discarding a spade from dummy. He now cashed the knave of hearts and this time discarded the nine of diamonds from dummy. Next came an avalanche of clubs to produce the following ending:

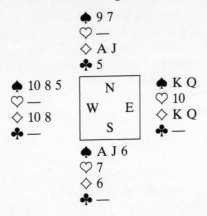

When dummy played the five of clubs East was caught in a triple squeeze and had to capitulate. If she throws a spade, South also throws a spade and cashes the ace and knave of spades thereby squeezing East in the red suits. If East throws a diamond, the ace and knave of diamonds are cashed and East is squeezed in the majors. Finally, if East parts with the ten of hearts, South cashes the ace of spades and seven of hearts, squeezing East in spades and diamonds.

Aunt Agatha complained bitterly about the result of this hand.

'There's no justice, absolutely none. Our game contract was vastly superior to Issie's daft 6NT, although I would have liked to have been in 6 ♣. The trouble about reaching a slam with my partner is that it takes a stick of dynamite to get her going. Mildred is so perpetually frightened of everything that it is not easy to get her to emerge from her forest of fear. Shrouded from head to foot in her own pessimism it's a wonder she ever makes a bid at all. And while I think of it, what were our other pair doing against 6NT? I'd like to see Issie make twelve tricks on a spade or diamond switch after the king of hearts.'

THE LAST SAY

It must be agreed, Aunt Agatha was very unlucky in this instance. As to West's defence against 6NT, a spade switch does not look like a good move when you consider the bidding. A diamond switch, however, is a plausible play, especially after East had contributed a low heart at trick one. Still, it would be far-sighted to calculate the real reason for this play—to break up the communications for the triple squeeze. In the end-game East would throw her ten of hearts, and then when the South hand was entered to cash the seven of hearts she could unguard her diamonds with impunity.

A few hands later Aunt Agatha was to suffer yet another adverse swing.

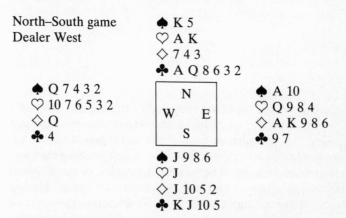

North–South game
Dealer West

♠ K 5
♡ A K
♢ 7 4 3
♣ A Q 8 6 3 2

♠ Q 7 4 3 2
♡ 10 7 6 5 3 2
♢ Q
♣ 4

N W E S

♠ A 10
♡ Q 9 8 4
♢ A K 9 8 6
♣ 9 7

♠ J 9 8 6
♡ J
♢ J 10 5 2
♣ K J 10 5

In Aunt Agatha's room the contract was 2 ♣ by North, making nine tricks—110 to Aunt Agatha.

In Issie's room this was the bidding, with Issie sitting South:

S	W	N	E
—	No	1 ♣	1 ◇
1 ♠	No	3 ♣	No
3NT	No	No	No

Against 3NT West led the queen of diamonds and, having held the trick, switched to the five of hearts. Dummy won, perforce, and after five club winners this was the position:

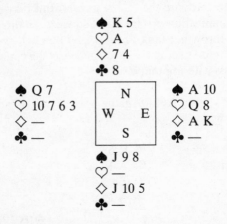

Although Issie could see only eight certain tricks (six clubs and two hearts), the eight of clubs from dummy now put considerable pressure on East. If she let the ten of spades go, Issie would play a low spade from dummy establishing the king. If she parted with one of her diamond honours, then a diamond lead would establish two diamond tricks for South. Having given the matter much thought, East discarded the eight of hearts, but Issie was in complete command. He now cashed the ace of hearts and threw East in with the king of diamonds. East was able to take one more diamond trick and the ace of spades, but then had to concede the king of spades to Issie for his ninth trick.

Again Aunt Agatha complained bitterly about Issie's

phenomenal luck, pointing out that all West had to do was to play the fourth highest of her longest and strongest suit ('Some books actually recommend this lead, you know, Freddie') and South would have been scuppered. True, but East had made a bid, and the same books also recommend leading partner's suit. At least when things go wrong after leading partner's suit you are better placed in the post-mortem than when you ignore partner and embark on some unsuccessful line of your own.

THE LAST SAY

What a curious hand this is! In theory there is no game contract on, which lends some support to Mildred's wishy-washy approach (remember, she played in 2 ♣). Also, it is very difficult to hit the only playable spot which offers some hope of game. Certainly South's 3NT rebid over 3 ♣ is not *that* obvious. Finally, seldom have I seen a player so severely punished as West for doing what seems the natural and obvious thing to do—leading partner's suit. Suppose the full lay-out had been more in keeping with the bidding, like this:

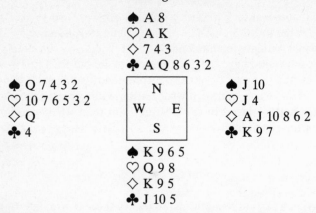

Can you imagine how West would have felt at the end of this hand, having led a heart, as East acidly enquired whether she had perhaps failed to hear her overcall of one diamond?

Issie had been having a short successful spell, but Aunt Agatha restored the balance to some extent on the following hand.

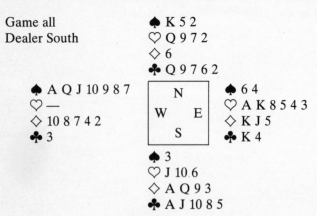

The bidding:

S	W	N	E
(A.A.)			
1 ♣	4 ♠	5 ♣	Dble
No	No	No	

West led the ace of spades and continued with the queen. The king of spades won the second trick, South discarding a heart, but the problem of turning two heart losers into one still remained. However, Aunt Agatha was not stymied for long. She realized that she would need both minor-suit kings right if she was to have any chance of success, so she ran the nine of clubs at trick three. When everyone followed, the nine holding, she played a diamond to the queen, ruffed a diamond, cashed the ace of clubs and ace of diamonds and ruffed her last diamond. This was the five-card ending, with North to play, West having been counted for seven spades (presumably), five diamonds and one club:

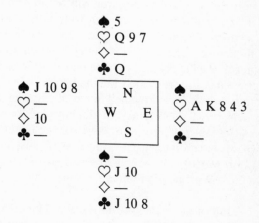

With the sweet smell of success in her nostrils, Aunt Agatha called for dummy's five of spades. The ten of hearts was discarded on this trick, and the knave of hearts on the next, when West was forced to concede a ruff and discard.

The comments at the conclusion of this hand were really quite funny but by no means without precedent in this class of bridge. West wanted to know why on earth East had doubled when she couldn't take a single trick. East replied, with some justification, that she had the best hand at the table. However, she was on less firm ground when she complained about her partner's ineptitude in failing to switch to a heart—a point which did not escape West's notice.

THE LAST SAY

Something that seemed to escape everyone's notice was that Aunt Agatha actually misplayed this hand—despite the fact that she made her contract. Suppose East covers the nine of clubs with the king. Now declarer will be an entry short to complete her elimination before throwing West on lead. The simple solution, of course, is to take the diamond finesse before the club finesse. Then when dummy is re-entered with a diamond ruff the king of clubs can be picked up with impunity.

I suppose it is also true to say that had West been sufficiently inspired she would have switched to a trump at trick two. This denies declarer a quick entry to dummy and consequently produces the same effect as East covering the nine of clubs at trick two. However, it is hard to criticize West. Just imagine the uproar there would have been had East's six of spades been a singleton and West not continued the suit!

And the result of the match? Aunt Agatha claimed a clear-cut win since she finished three imps to the good. Issie claimed a draw since the margin was inconclusive, and both sides were adamant that their opponents had had all the luck.

3

A Basket at the
Puddlewick Congress

Why don't I keep my big mouth shut? If I hadn't told Aunt Agatha about the basket—or rather the lack of it—I might never have been cornered. But it had been one of those days: bills galore, the annual tax return, a polite message from my bank manager inviting me to go and see him (no prizes for guessing what that meant) and many tedious letters . . . and the only waste-paper basket I had was full. Full and overflowing. I happened to mention this to Aunt Agatha on the phone . . .

'My dear boy,' she said, 'I know exactly what to do. You really need a break. We'll go to the Puddlewick Congress together and *win* a basket.'

'But we'd need at least a couple of firsts, Aunt Agatha. You know how pathetic bridge prizes are in this country,' I replied, exaggerating a little but desperately trying to find some straw to cling to.

'I don't want to listen to excuses,' retorted my aunt firmly, 'and in any case why shouldn't we win two firsts? You don't play *so* badly. I'll make all the arrangements. Take it as fixed.' I did, and I was.

I have heard of some odd reasons for playing bridge at a congress—usually concerning the opposite sex—but never anything quite so ludicrous as having a basket as the prime target, although, with that indefinable sense of logic that many women proffer with such compelling charm, Aunt Agatha could see nothing strange in our quest.

'Sure to be plenty of baskets there,' she said, with one of her rare attempts at humour.

Having set the scene, here we are with the first prize exhibit.

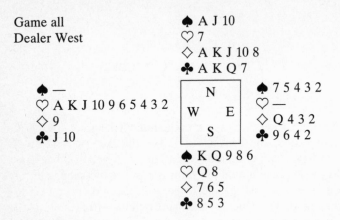

Game all
Dealer West

```
                    ♠ A J 10
                    ♡ 7
                    ◇ A K J 10 8
                    ♣ A K Q 7
♠ —                                    ♠ 7 5 4 3 2
♡ A K J 10 9 6 5 4 3 2        N        ♡ —
◇ 9                      W         E    ◇ Q 4 3 2
♣ J 10                        S        ♣ 9 6 4 2
                    ♠ K Q 9 8 6
                    ♡ Q 8
                    ◇ 7 6 5
                    ♣ 8 5 3
```

The bidding:

S	W	N	E
	(A.A.)		(F.N.)
—	4 ♡	Dble	No
4 ♠	No	5 ♡	No
6 ♠	No	No	No

Aunt Agatha likes to call a spade a spade and that is why she bid 4 ♡, if you see what I mean. With such a freak hand more devious minds might pass initially and then emerge from the undergrowth later on hoping to buy the contract cheaply. Such tactics, however, are not usually in the Aunt Agatha repertoire.

Against 6 ♠ Aunt Agatha led the ace of hearts, and I discarded a small diamond. She continued with the king of hearts and already I was in big trouble. A second diamond discard or a small club would have been equally fatal, so I did the best I could for the moment by underruffing! However, declarer did not take long to find the winning line of play. The ace of spades followed by the ace of clubs, the ace and king of diamonds and the knave of spades overtaken by the queen gave South the lead to draw the last two trumps. This was the four-card ending:

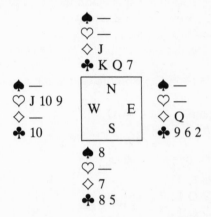

On the last spade dummy parted with the knave of diamonds. I was squeezed, declarer was beaming, and Aunt Agatha looked daggers at everyone in turn. She was obviously not completely happy about my underruff at trick two, although she must have had her suspicions that I was trapped, because she made only a token attack and then quickly insisted that we get on with the next board.

THE LAST SAY

It would be churlish to criticize Aunt Agatha for playing a second heart because most of us would do exactly that, and take some persuading that we had erred in any way. Nevertheless, the slam must fail if West switches. It matters not whether she chooses a club or a diamond. The effect is the same.

To stand any chance declarer will have to come to hand with a trump in order to ruff the queen of hearts, but this time it will no longer be necessary for East to underruff. Any minor suit can be discarded with impunity. Struggle as he may, declarer will have to concede defeat.

Another interesting point is that if East's trumps are headed by the eight, instead of the seven, it is a completely different ball game. Now he can afford to be squeezed, and even enjoy it. That eight of spades is more than adequate compensation.

We seemed to be unlucky on the next hand of note.

East–West game
Dealer North

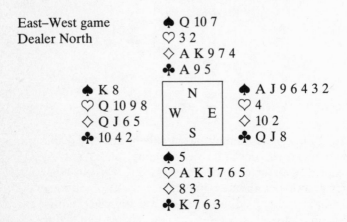

♠ Q 10 7
♡ 3 2
♢ A K 9 7 4
♣ A 9 5

♠ K 8
♡ Q 10 9 8
♢ Q J 6 5
♣ 10 4 2

♠ A J 9 6 4 3 2
♡ 4
♢ 10 2
♣ Q J 8

♠ 5
♡ A K J 7 6 5
♢ 8 3
♣ K 7 6 3

The bidding:

S	W (A.A.)	N	E (F.N.)
—	—	1NT	2 ♠
4 ♡	Dble	No	No
No			

Aunt Agatha led the king and another spade. Declarer ruffed the second round, cashed the ace of hearts, the ace and king of diamonds and ruffed a diamond. Now the ace of clubs, a second diamond ruff and the king of clubs left this position—the defence having taken just one trick:

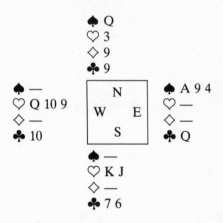

South led a club, and I had the unenviable task of end-playing Aunt Agatha on the next trick, all because South was cad enough to discard a club on my ace of spades.

THE LAST SAY

With hindsight, it is easy to say that Aunt Agatha should not have doubled. Left to his own devices South might have handled the trump suit differently, but it would have been totally out of character for Aunt Agatha to pass 4 ♡ once I had opened my mouth. As she said herself, 'It was pairs, after all, and how was I to know that that cretinous individual would actually play the hand with a degree of intelligence?'

Our poor run continued, and on the next board we scored a complete zero.

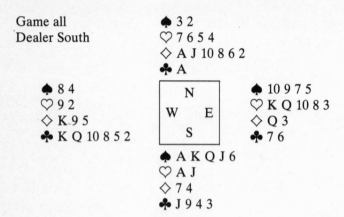

Game all

Dealer South

The bidding:

S	W	N	E
(A.A.)		(F.N.)	
1 ♠	2 ♣	2 ♦	No
2NT	No	3NT	No
No	No		

West led the king of clubs against Aunt Agatha's contract of 3NT. Entering her hand with the ace of spades, Aunt Agatha led a diamond. West, naturally, hopped up with the king and Aunt Agatha, naturally, gave West a dirty look and ducked. West now switched to the nine of hearts, East contributing the queen and Aunt Agatha the ace. At this point no doubt Aunt Agatha should have cashed her spade winners, but she was anxious to get on with the diamond suit and duly played a second round. West followed with the nine, dummy the ten and East the queen. Four rounds of hearts came next. This was the position before the fifth heart was cashed:

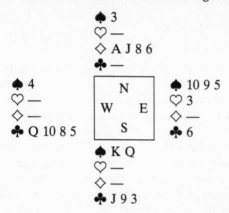

♠ 3
♡ —
◇ A J 8 6
♣ —

♠ 4   ♠ 10 9 5
♡ —   ♡ 3
◇ —   ◇ —
♣ Q 10 8 5   ♣ 6

♠ K Q
♡ —
◇ —
♣ J 9 3

On the three of hearts Aunt Agatha had to throw the queen of spades in order to avoid losing the rest of the tricks. West craftily threw a club. Now East played the six of clubs to the nine and ten leaving West to complete the slaughter by exiting with the carefully preserved four of spades. Of course West took the last two tricks and that was +500 to his side, Aunt Agatha having collected no more than four tricks.

'If you'd passed 2NT I would have made my contract,' observed Aunt Agatha. This gem of wisdom might or might not have been true, but it certainly showed that Aunt Agatha had not yet directed her mind to the hand as a whole. She continued, 'Once the diamonds behaved badly your hand was useless to me. In fact you could have chucked it in the waste-paper basket.'

'Talking of waste-paper baskets, Aunt Agatha—' I began.

'Yes, yes, I know,' retorted my aunt irritably. 'Our bad luck can't go on for ever. Sooner or later these cripples we have for opponents must surely stop playing like Belladonna and Garozzo rolled into one.'

THE LAST SAY

With eight tricks on top one can normally find a ninth and it is a little unusual to finish up with only four. Certainly Aunt Agatha's handling of the dummy left something to be desired; but full marks to West, who found a classy defence. Hopping up with the king of diamonds was unquestionably the right play (the idea is to force declarer either to win the trick prematurely, thereby destroying his communications, or duck and perhaps not win a trick in the suit at all). Although West's sabotaging tactics endangered East's queen of diamonds it was the only play to keep the defence alive.

Just as I was beginning to think that my lovely new waste-paper basket was getting irremediably out of reach, Aunt Agatha gave a scintillating performance to recover from another 'Bellarozzo' defence. This must surely be the turning-point, I thought to myself.

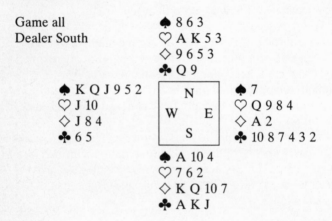

```
Game all              ♠ 8 6 3
Dealer South          ♡ A K 5 3
                      ◇ 9 6 5 3
                      ♣ Q 9
        ♠ K Q J 9 5 2     N        ♠ 7
        ♡ J 10                     ♡ Q 9 8 4
        ◇ J 8 4       W       E    ◇ A 2
        ♣ 6 5                      ♣ 10 8 7 4 3 2
                          S
                      ♠ A 10 4
                      ♡ 7 6 2
                      ◇ K Q 10 7
                      ♣ A K J
```

The bidding:

S	W	N	E
(A.A.)		(F.N.)	
1 ◇	No	1 ♡	No
2NT	No	3NT	No
No	No		

The contract was the same at most tables. Usually West mentioned his spades, but sometimes, as against us, he decided not to bid. In any case the play followed routine lines. West led the king of spades, which was allowed to win. The spade continuation was won by South, who then entered dummy twice to lead diamonds. In this manner the successful declarers came to nine tricks via one spade, three diamonds, two hearts and three clubs.

At our table Aunt Agatha encountered a rather more resourceful defender in the East seat than most of the other declarers had experienced. At trick two, on the queen of spades, he discarded the ace of diamonds! Aunt Agatha was clearly a little put out by this development and scowled darkly at East, who nevertheless went through the motions of pretending not to notice.

Having given this sinister development some thought Aunt Agatha came to two firm conclusions. One, it wasn't Christmas. Two, East was not just a benign, kindly old gentleman who wanted to help her on her way. She therefore won the second trick with her ace of spades, cashed the king of diamonds, the king of hearts, the three top clubs and the ace of hearts.

In order to protect the knave of diamonds West was forced to part with a spade. Aunt Agatha now exited with a spade, and West had to concede the last two diamonds to her Q 10.

Aunt Agatha was naturally delighted with her card reading, and managing to thwart East's Machiavellian plot gave her immense satisfaction. We still hadn't scored a top, but with my aunt in this form the writing was surely on the wall.

THE LAST SAY

In retrospect it occurred to me what a coup East might have effected had the East–West cards been altered slightly. Suppose they had been like this:

♠ K Q J 9 5 2	N	♠ 7
♡ J 10 4	W E	♡ Q 9 8
◇ 8 4	S	◇ A J 2
♣ 6 5		♣ 10 8 7 4 3 2

West still discards a spade on the third round of clubs, just as though he had a real problem guarding the diamonds, but then the roof will cave in completely when he produces the third heart for a one-trick set.

I can't wait to try that coup some time when I am a defender. Throwing away an ace, as if your middle name was Rothschild, gives many players a deep sense of satisfaction. But throwing away an ace which then misleads declarer into going for a non-existent end-play—now that is something. I must give it a name. How about the 'Anti-Agatha Coup'?

Our first top was gained in an unusual way. I'm sure it came about because some joker had one look at Aunt Agatha and decided that here was an old duck who was just asking to be mugged. Foolish, foolish man! Like so many before him, he soon found out that Aunt Agatha is especially deadly when countering what she regards as a vicious attack. Somehow she seems to sense the moment when a low punch is about to be delivered and has that happy knack of not only countering it but hitting back where it hurts most. Moral: never try to mug my aunt. She doesn't always adhere to the Queensberry Rules when retaliating.

Love all
Dealer North

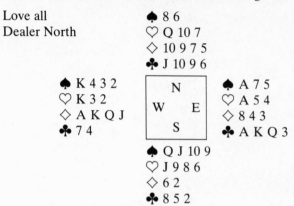

♠ 8 6
♡ Q 10 7
♢ 10 9 7 5
♣ J 10 9 6

♠ K 4 3 2
♡ K 3 2
♢ A K Q J
♣ 7 4

♠ A 7 5
♡ A 5 4
♢ 8 4 3
♣ A K Q 3

♠ Q J 10 9
♡ J 9 8 6
♢ 6 2
♣ 8 5 2

The bidding:

S	W (A.A.)	N	E (F.N.)
—	—	No	1 ♣
1NT	Dble	No	No
No			

Considering the vulnerability, you may agree that this was a remarkable sequence. Anyway, Aunt Agatha cashed her four top diamonds and switched to a club. I won with the queen and returned a low spade, brilliantly ducked by Aunt Agatha to rectify the count for a possible squeeze. South continued spades, the position being projected to the following four-card ending:

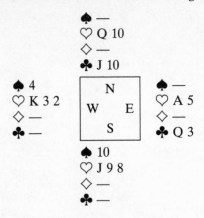

```
            ♠ —
            ♡ Q 10
            ◇ —
            ♣ J 10

♠ 4           N          ♠ —
♡ K 3 2                  ♡ A 5
◇ —       W       E      ◇ —
♣ —           S          ♣ Q 3

            ♠ 10
            ♡ J 9 8
            ◇ —
            ♣ —
```

It is East to lead and you'll notice that North has already been forced to unguard the heart suit. When I led the queen of clubs South could no longer retain control in both majors. So that was +1,100 to East–West.

Without the defence ducking a spade the penalty might well have been only 900, and that would have been a ghastly result compared with the 990 scored by all those East–West pairs who had bid and made 6NT. Of course, it was easier for the declarers to read the squeeze ending than for Aunt Agatha, and a number of them had found their way home. Still, not all the East-West pairs were appreciative of our result. One Gallic couple, no doubt recalling Marshall Bosquet's famous comment on the Charge of the Light Brigade, were heard to say, '*C'est magnifique, mais ce n'est pas le bridge.*'

THE LAST SAY

The coup that South tried to perpetrate on this hand is more commonly encountered at favourable vulnerability, where it is a little easier to gauge the profit and loss account. Ideally, you

hope to be doubled, stand your ground and find there is no way
to take a trick.

I believe the first person to exploit this coup with spectacular
success was Terence Reese back in the fifties. This was a hand
that Jeremy Flint and I recorded in *Tiger Bridge*, from the 1951
British Trials.

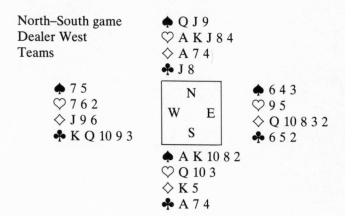

North–South game
Dealer West
Teams

♠ Q J 9
♡ A K J 8 4
◇ A 7 4
♣ J 8

♠ 7 5
♡ 7 6 2
◇ J 9 6
♣ K Q 10 9 3

♠ 6 4 3
♡ 9 5
◇ Q 10 8 3 2
♣ 6 5 2

♠ A K 10 8 2
♡ Q 10 3
◇ K 5
♣ A 7 4

The bidding:

S	W	N	E
			(Reese)
—	No	1 ♡	1NT
Dble	No	No	No

Although declarer played the hand with his customary skill,
he failed to make a single trick, which, of course, was highly
satisfactory. Seven down cost his side 1,300, but that was a mere
flea-bite compared with the 2,220 scored by his team-mates in
the other room.

On the next hand Aunt Agatha, now South, earned maximum
points again with a fine exhibition of dummy play.

Game all
Dealer North

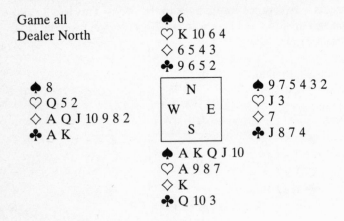

```
                        ♠ 6
                        ♡ K 10 6 4
                        ◇ 6 5 4 3
                        ♣ 9 6 5 2
  ♠ 8                    ┌─────────┐         ♠ 9 7 5 4 3 2
  ♡ Q 5 2                │    N    │         ♡ J 3
  ◇ A Q J 10 9 8 2       │  W   E  │         ◇ 7
  ♣ A K                  │    S    │         ♣ J 8 7 4
                        └─────────┘
                        ♠ A K Q J 10
                        ♡ A 9 8 7
                        ◇ K
                        ♣ Q 10 3
```

The bidding:

S (A.A.)	W	N (F.N.)	E
—	—	No	No
1 ♠	Dble	No	2 ♣
2 ♡	4 ◇	4 ♡	No
No	Dble	No	No
No			

Perhaps my bid of 4 ♡ was not all that well judged (Aunt
Agatha describes it in less charitable terms!), but it wasn't *so*
obvious to double 4 ◇.

Despite having four losers on top (2 clubs, 1 diamond and 1
heart), Aunt Agatha managed to concede only three tricks to
her somewhat bewildered opponents. Looking back on this
hand, when the dust of battle had finally settled and the result
was safely in the bag, I was able to claim that I had gone for the

gold rather than the silver. In the circumstances it wasn't easy, even for Aunt Agatha, to knock my assertion.

This was how the play proceeded. West cashed the ace and king of clubs and followed with the ace and queen of diamonds. Aunt Agatha ruffed the fourth trick in her hand, East discarding a spade, and played the ace and king of spades. West couldn't ruff without giving the contract, so he discarded a diamond and dummy parted with a club. A third and fourth spade were won in hand, while West discarded diamonds and dummy a second, and last, club and a diamond. Now the ten of spades was ruffed in dummy, West discarding yet another diamond, and the six of diamonds ruffed in hand. It did not help East to trump so he discarded a club.

This was the position: South to lead, having lost three tricks.

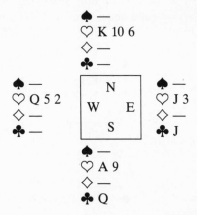

```
              ♠ —
              ♡ K 10 6
              ◇ —
              ♣ —
  ♠ —          ┌─────────┐      ♠ —
  ♡ Q 5 2      │   N     │      ♡ J 3
  ◇ —          │ W   E   │      ◇ —
  ♣ —          │   S     │      ♣ J
               └─────────┘
              ♠ —
              ♡ A 9
              ◇ —
              ♣ Q
```

When Aunt Agatha led the queen of clubs West did his best by contributing the queen of hearts, but Aunt Agatha was not to be denied her moment of glory as she won with the king and then successfully finessed against East's knave. Plus 790 was a blissful sight on the score-sheet.

THE LAST SAY

Aunt Agatha was so pleased at making her contract that she was
almost prepared to forgive me for failing to punish 4 ◇. You'll
observe that this contract fails by one trick providing North–
South are careful not to open up the heart suit. When declarer
has to tackle hearts himself, he must lose three tricks in the suit,
plus a spade, for a total loss of 200. However, thanks to the
Devil's Coup—that was the coup Aunt Agatha introduced to
make one of her trump losers vanish—there was no doubt
which contract produced the better score. That was a powerful
weapon I used to some purpose in the post-mortem.

It's curious how a doubtful bidding sequence can sometimes
reward a partnership quite undeservedly. This happened on the
following hand:

Game all   ♠ A 5
Dealer South   ♡ A K Q 3
                       ◇ A K Q J 8 4
                       ♣ 3

```
        N
   W        E
        S
```

                       ♠ Q 8 7 4 3
                       ♡ 4
                       ◇ 10 9 7 5
                       ♣ K 10 6

The bidding:

S	W	N	E
(A.A.)		(F.N.)	
No	No	2 ♣	No
2 ♦	No	3 ♦	No
3 ♠	No	4 ♡	No
5 ♣	Dble	5 ♦	No
6 ♦	No	No	No

'The big bull point about this hand,' explained my aunt quite solemnly a little later on, 'was that I was going to be declarer.' And then as an afterthought, possibly reading my 'inscrutable' expression, 'I mean, the lead was coming up to me.' Just as she seemed to put our relationship back on an even keel again she gave the knife a final twist by saying, 'Although, of course, a woman's intuition *is* so much better than a man's.'

Before we see how Aunt Agatha set about making her contract, how would you plan the play when West leads the ten of hearts?

At most tables North–South either didn't bid a slam or else went down in one, so success was certain to reap a fine reward. At a cursory glance declarer may decide that his best chance is to find East with the ace of clubs so that a discard can be established for dummy's losing spade. Thus South will make six diamonds, three hearts and a ruff, one spade and one club. However, this was the full deal:

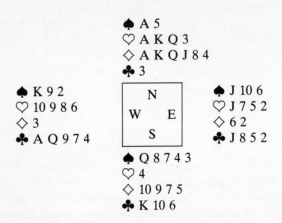

Thinking back to the bidding, Aunt Agatha reasoned that West was likely to hold the ace of clubs, and therefore she would need a more sophisticated plan than leading a club from dummy towards her king. So, she won the heart lead in dummy, drew trumps, cashed the top hearts, discarding clubs from hand, and ruffed a heart. This was the position with South to play:

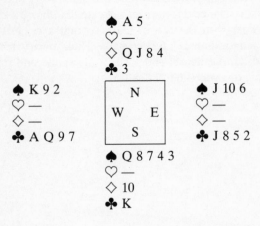

Aunt Agatha now played the king of clubs, giving West the option of conceding a ruff and discard or leading away from his king of spades. How did she know that West had the king of spades, you may ask? That's easy: if East held it there was no play for the contract, so West *had* to have it. Aunt Agatha believes in positive thinking, so as far as she was concerned the issue was never in doubt!

THE LAST SAY

The doubtful bid in our sequence—or at least one of them—was Aunt Agatha's 5 ♣. She intended it to mean, 'I like diamonds and have a club feature.' I thought she was agreeing hearts and probably held the ace of clubs. Something like: ♠ Q x x x x; ♡ J x x x; ♢ x x; ♣ A x. Whatever her intentions, it seemed to me that it wouldn't hurt to emphasize the diamonds *en route* to wherever it was we were going. When she converted to 6 ♢ the mist cleared—well, sort of.

I suppose it was tempting for West to shriek about his clubs but such bids are liable to rebound and hit the defenders in the face. Declarer, on the other hand, stands to gain considerably from all free and accurate information and, as we have seen, this was an expensive piece of chit-chat from West. Had he kept quiet it is almost certain that Aunt Agatha would have gone down.

In West's defence perhaps it should be said that he also thought the final contract was going to be played in hearts by North. That being the case he wanted his partner to lead a club. He has a point there.

The next hand illustrates Aunt Agatha in dazzling form once more.

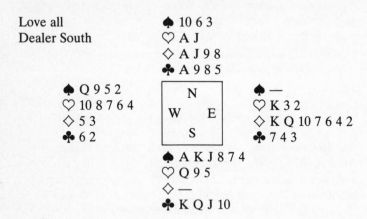

Love all   ♠ 10 6 3
Dealer South   ♡ A J
               ◇ A J 9 8
               ♣ A 9 8 5

♠ Q 9 5 2   ♠ —
♡ 10 8 7 6 4   ♡ K 3 2
◇ 5 3   ◇ K Q 10 7 6 4 2
♣ 6 2   ♣ 7 4 3

               ♠ A K J 8 7 4
               ♡ Q 9 5
               ◇ —
               ♣ K Q J 10

The bidding:

S	W	N	E
(A.A.)		(F.N.)	
2 ♠	No	3 ♠	4 ◇
4 ♠	No	5 ♣	No
5 ◇	No	6 ♠	No
No	No		

West led the five of diamonds, and again Aunt Agatha seems to be faced with two inescapable losers: the queen of spades and the king of hearts. However, the diamond was ducked in dummy and East's ten ruffed by South. The ace of spades and a small spade gave West the lead once more, East discarding the seven of diamonds and the three of clubs. No doubt West should have picked up her partner's message (how else could he shriek for a heart?), but she woodenly continued with the three of diamonds. This time Aunt Agatha played the ace of diamonds from dummy, discarded the ten of clubs from her

hand and drew trumps. On the fourth round of trumps Aunt
Agatha discarded dummy's knave of hearts. Three rounds of
clubs followed, dummy's ace winning the third round, to leave
this position:

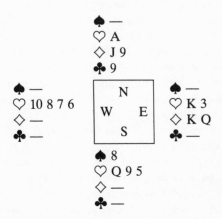

The nine of clubs, on which Aunt Agatha threw the five of
hearts, caught East in a ruffing squeeze. If he played his small
heart, Aunt Agatha would cash the ace of hearts leaving her
hand high. If he threw a diamond, a diamond ruff would leave
dummy high.

'Why didn't you switch to a heart, partner?' demanded East,
annoyed that his message had not got through.

'If you had discarded a high one I would have done so,'
retorted West, who obviously hadn't followed the subtle
inferences of East's discards.

'And how high is the three, or did you want me to discard the
king?' enquired East petulantly.

THE LAST SAY

No doubt you have noticed that 6 ♣ by North is ironclad, but not so easy to reach after a 2 ♠ opening—especially at pairs.

As to the defence, it is surprising how many players take scant notice of the small cards, although only too often they are the sole medium of communication. Short of standing on his head in the middle of the table, East did everything in his power to alert his partner to the importance of a heart switch. But his seven of diamonds, when he could well have played the two or the four, meant nothing to West. More inquisitive Wests would have wondered why East had discarded the *highest diamond he could afford.* On mature reflection it could only be a McKenney signal for a heart switch. The three of clubs only served to corroborate what East had already said. Unnecessary, it's true, but some partners can't have enough first-class nursing if they are to keep out of trouble and sometimes find the winning line. The fact that West still erred takes nothing away from East, who did his Florence Nightingale act with commendable efficiency.

As we moved to the next table Aunt Agatha was giving a fine impression of the cat that had just polished off the last of the cream. And the next hand did nothing to deflate her ebullience.

Love all
Dealer South

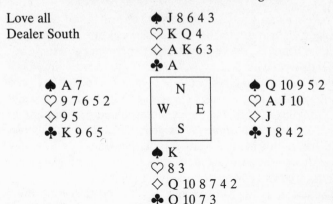

♠ J 8 6 4 3
♡ K Q 4
◇ A K 6 3
♣ A

♠ A 7
♡ 9 7 6 5 2
◇ 9 5
♣ K 9 6 5

♠ Q 10 9 5 2
♡ A J 10
◇ J
♣ J 8 4 2

♠ K
♡ 8 3
◇ Q 10 8 7 4 2
♣ Q 10 7 3

The bidding:

S	W	N	E
(A.A.)		(F.N.)	
No	No	1 ♠	No
2 ◇	No	4 ♣	No
4 ◇	No	5 ◇	No
No	No		

My bid of 4 ♣ agreed diamonds and showed slam interest,
which was something that Aunt Agatha was anxious to
discourage. She was a little below strength for her first response
so had some reason to be apprehensive. I took the hint and
settled for the diamond game, but was full of misgivings until it
became clear that 3NT must fail against routine defence. Hands
like this are always a nightmare for pairs players: if you by-pass
3NT all may be well if you have a minor-suit slam to bid, but if
game is the limit you all too often want to return to 3NT for an
easier nine-trick contract, and maybe land the magic ten for a
top award of 430.

West led the ace and another spade. How should Aunt
Agatha play? Also, how should East defend when a heart is led
to the king?

Aunt Agatha could see ten tricks, assuming the diamonds were not all in one hand. Six diamonds, one club, two club ruffs and one heart. Prospects for the extra trick were good: the ace of hearts with West or the development of an extra winner from one of the black suits. There was also the possibility of a squeeze if East held the ace of hearts and a link to the suit could be maintained. Thinking about these points, and wanting to give East every opportunity to exit comfortably if he did in fact hold the ace of hearts, Aunt Agatha played a heart at trick three. Just as she anticipated, East took dummy's king of hearts with the ace and exited with the two of clubs.

The ace and king of diamonds now forced East to throw a heart. He can't afford a spade, otherwise dummy's fifth spade can be set up; and he can't afford a club, otherwise the knave can be pinned. With the opponents' trumps out of the way Aunt Agatha proceeded to crossruff her black suits. Spade ruff, club ruff, spade ruff and club ruff produced the following position, with dummy to play. Declarer has lost two tricks.

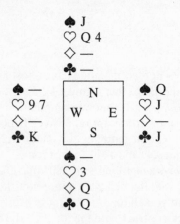

The knave of spades was ruffed in hand, and West had to shut up shop. Aunt Agatha positively beamed as she watched me write +400 on the score-sheet, a lone entry of that amount in the North–South column.

THE LAST SAY

Aunt Agatha had played well, there was no denying it, but there is an adage that you can only play as well as your opponents let you. In fact East was guilty of a costly defensive error when in with the ace of hearts. True, Aunt Agatha carefully refrained from reducing his options by playing a heart at trick three. Even so, exiting with a club was a lazy play. Had East ducked the king of hearts it might have worked, although the snag to this defence becomes apparent when East considers what he will discard should declarer continue with two top diamonds. In fact he is squeezed.

The best defence by far is for East to return a heart at trick four. His partner's two of hearts should have given him the count, and the point of this play is that it breaks the communication between declarer and dummy. Once the link has been severed there is no way that declarer can execute a squeeze, and the contract must fail.

Destroying the vital connecting link is a facet of defence that deserves far greater attention than it usually receives. An elementary understanding of squeeze technique is usually sufficient to alert a thoughtful defender to the possibilities. In this case it is not even necessary for East to know what sort of squeeze might take place, or who will be the victim. Once he addresses his mind to the question of cutting communications he will realize that there is only *one* link to be severed—the heart link. The other side suits are either blocked or cut already, so his problem is really quite simple.

When Aunt Agatha strikes form there is no holding her, and it is pleasing to record that she continued to leave a great deal of carnage in her wake. No doubt her file on the Puddlewick Congress has long since been closed, inscribed with the immortal words, 'Mission Accomplished'. Yes, I have to admit there has been an addition to my list of worldly goods and chattels. What the army would call: baskets, waste-paper, one. A handsome reminder of our epic struggle at Puddlewick.

4

*Aunt Agatha Plays
Despite the Computer*

It was clear from Aunt Agatha's demeanour that we were about
to hear some important news. She had gathered her clan around
her, and there was a note of expectancy in the air. It was
important *bad* news, I suspected. Perhaps her cat had died, or
her shares gone down with a bump, or maybe she was about to
give up bridge, sign the pledge or join a religious sect.
Speculation was rife in my mind as I pondered on the intriguing
possibilities.

'I know it will be tragic for everyone concerned,' began my
aunt when she was certain the stage was all hers.

'Oh dear,' I murmured, 'the family fortunes are in ruins.'

Giving me an icy look Aunt Agatha continued, after just the
right pause for dramatic effect, 'I shall be unable to accompany
you on your bridge cruise in November. Naturally, things won't
be the same without me, but I shall make it up to everyone on
the next cruise.'

Mamma mia! The sting was in the tail. Just as the 'bad news'
turned out to be like a waft of balmy summer air, so the 'good
news' was depressing. Still, the next cruise wasn't until May.
Perhaps Aunt Agatha would have forgotten all about it by then,
I told myself, consolingly if none too convincingly.

'The reason for this decision,' continued Aunt Agatha,
commanding everyone's attention again, 'is that I promised
Mildred I would play with her at the Maypole Hotel Congress. I
can't let her down. Besides, Issie and Sally are playing together
and we are going as a four.'

There was a moment's hush as the assembled company

assimilated this world-shattering news item and no doubt conjured up a picture of the quartet descending on the unsuspecting Maypole Hotel. It was a safe bet that Aunt Agatha would unleash a few surprises for them all before she finally took her leave.

'Of course, we shall have to suffer at the hands of their wretched computer,' complained my aunt. She hated computer-dealt hands and, just as though we didn't know her views already, she launched forth into a violent diatribe on the subject.

'Computerized deals,' she announced with considerable venom, 'are an absolute menace to *real* bridge players.' At that moment there was an untimely interruption.

'But Harold Franklin says—' The interpolator was Issie, but we never did hear what it was that Harold Franklin said.

With a withering look at Issie, Aunt Agatha quickly took up the running again. 'I don't care if Harold Wilson says . . . I believe my eyes, they don't deceive me. No doubt it is a wonderful idea in theory—so was Frankenstein, which is just what the computer should be called. Maybe tournament directors like the hands fixed this way; maybe they are the only rational answer when there are enormous entries; but nobody will ever convince me that the end-product is not invariably a wild and maniacal mixture of goulash and Russian roulette. And anyone who actually enjoys that sort of concoction would do well to retire from bridge and set course for the nearest casino.'

Apparently Aunt Agatha's allergy to computer-dealt hands arose as a result of playing at the Maypole Hotel Congress the previous year. This is a very popular congress, and huge entries had been received. Playing with Mildred, Aunt Agatha had sat East–West in the first session and it seemed to her that eight-card suits and voids had appeared with—as she put it—'Even greater frequency than Zsa Zsa Gabor collects husbands.'

All the hands had been created by Frankenstein, the computer, and although they did not meet with my aunt's approval, no one, even in their wildest dreams, would have described them as lacking in colour. Conservatively, they were coquettish, although I know that was not Aunt Agatha's choice of word. However, it was not everyone that complained—not by a long chalk. Issie, partnering Sally, thoroughly enjoyed playing North–South. While Aunt Agatha was particularly bitter about the bad breaks and incredible distributions that came her way, it seems that Issie bid everything in sight, doubled every opponent out of sight and generally scattered mayhem in all directions.

Let us look at some of those hands that caused Aunt Agatha such anguish and Issie such joy. But remember, although Issie was clearly rather lucky from time to time, he often engineered his good fortune—admittedly sometimes by methods that would hardly have received the seal of approval from the expert establishment.

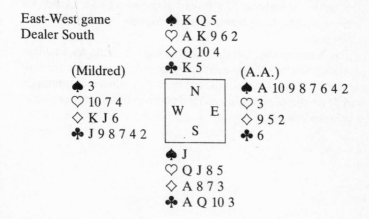

East-West game
Dealer South

(Mildred)

(A.A.)

♠ K Q 5
♡ A K 9 6 2
♢ Q 10 4
♣ K 5

♠ 3
♡ 10 7 4
♢ K J 6
♣ J 9 8 7 4 2

♠ A 10 9 8 7 6 4 2
♡ 3
♢ 9 5 2
♣ 6

♠ J
♡ Q J 8 5
♢ A 8 7 3
♣ A Q 10 3

At Aunt Agatha's table the opponents' bidding was smoothly efficient:

S	N
1 ♡	4NT
5 ♡	6 ♡

So, although Aunt Agatha held one of her famous, or possibly infamous, eight-card suits, she had not been able to get a word in. That sort of thing tends to frustrate Aunt Agatha, as she is garrulous by nature, and sitting quietly saying nothing is just not her scene.

Although lacking guidance from Aunt Agatha, Mildred did not have to be a genius to lead the three of spades, nor her partner to try to give her a ruff. Obligingly South discarded a small diamond. But wait . . . the party was not yet over. Declarer still had to find a way of avoiding a two-trick set, for what was he to do with two losing diamonds unless the knave of clubs fell?

Recovering from the shock of having his spade trick ruffed, declarer won the trump continuation in dummy, drew trumps, cashed the ace of diamonds and the black-suit kings, and then ran down the hearts. This was the position before dummy's last heart was played:

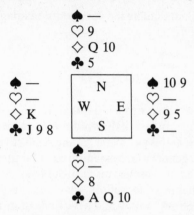

On the nine of hearts West found it impossible to retain control of the minors and comply with the requirement that she should play a card. Yes, Mildred had been well and truly squeezed, and the declarer had managed to hold his losses to one down.

'I suppose we had to have a genius at the wheel,' muttered Aunt Agatha disparagingly as she peered over the travelling score-sheet. Quite a few North–South pairs had lost 100 (6 ♡–2), which didn't exactly please my aunt. However, Issie helped to improve Aunt Agatha's score when he and Sally also bid to 6 ♡, after exactly the same auction. Again the three of spades was led, East winning and returning a spade. But now Issie ruffed with the queen of hearts and then, projecting the end-game to the position already shown, proceeded to make his contract. Bravo, Issie!

Talking about this hand later on it became clear that Issie's apparent brilliance was perhaps overshadowed by his respect for the computer.

'In the normal way,' he explained, 'I would have discarded a diamond at trick two, but there had not been a hand with an eight-card suit for a couple of deals or so, therefore I knew one was about due. I thought I would ruff and see what happened.

The Vienna Coup and squeeze were automatic after that,' he added modestly.

THE LAST SAY

A curious point about this hand is that the queen of spades is a complete mirage. In fact, it does nothing to make declarer's life any easier, and in this particular setting seems to adopt the role of Circe, the legendary Greek temptress. Our first declarer was tempted and fell for a useless discard, but Issie, no doubt having heard what happens to sailors who are tempted (and so, perhaps, professors too), would have none of it. Although this was an admirable decision it was of course made for quite the wrong reason! He didn't ruff as a safety measure and because the discard would be useless anyway; he ruffed because his abacus, or whatever, told him that it was time for another eight-card suit to appear and he didn't expect West to let him enjoy the discard.

On firmer ground, note Issie's good technique in cashing the ace of diamonds (Vienna Coup) so as to avoid a blockage when the heart winners started to bite.

Another freak hand resulted in a poor score for Aunt Agatha and Mildred when their opponents refused to go quietly. This was the deal:

East–West game
Dealer East

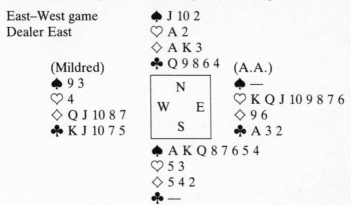

♠ J 10 2
♡ A 2
◇ A K 3
♣ Q 9 8 6 4

(Mildred)
♠ 9 3
♡ 4
◇ Q J 10 8 7
♣ K J 10 7 5

(A.A.)
♠ —
♡ K Q J 10 9 8 7 6
◇ 9 6
♣ A 3 2

♠ A K Q 8 7 6 5 4
♡ 5 3
◇ 5 4 2
♣ —

As Aunt Agatha was the dealer there was no question of her being silenced on this occasion, but her opening gambit of 4 ♡ was soon smothered by South's 4 ♠. North raised to 6 ♠ and that was the final contract.

Mildred saw no good reason to find a 'fancy lead', as she put it, and laid down the four of hearts.

Well, what do you think? Should declarer make his contract or not?

In practice South did not find the hand particularly testing. He won with the ace of hearts, ruffed a club and entered dummy twice with spades to ruff two more clubs. He then exited with his small heart. East switched to the nine of diamonds, but declarer won in dummy, ruffed a fourth club and played his penultimate trump to reach this position:

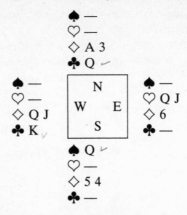

When the queen of spades appeared Mildred was squeezed for the second time in the space of a few hands. She accepted this treatment philosophically enough as South entered +980 on the score-sheet, but Aunt Agatha was not so generous. My aunt takes it as a personal insult if somebody squeezes her, and regards it as only a slightly less heinous offence to squeeze her partner.

Suddenly Aunt Agatha's eyes narrowed as she looked more closely at the mechanics required for the squeeze.

'You know, Mildred, if only you had led the top of your sequence, the queen of diamonds, he could never have made his contract. The squeeze gets broken up when he ducks a trick to rectify the count. I would return a diamond and that completely scuppers him.'

Mildred looked crestfallen at the implied criticism, but perked up a little as she trotted out one of her beloved clichés.

'Oh, I *had* to lead your suit, my dear, especially as it was a singleton.'

Well, let's see what happened at Issie's table where he, too, was in 6 ♠. This time the West player did not hold quite such rigid views as Mildred. She reasoned that there was not much prospect of doing anything with the heart suit, so she led the queen of diamonds.

Issie won with the ace of diamonds and ruffed a club. He then entered dummy twice more with trumps and each time ruffed clubs. When the ace of clubs fell it seemed unlikely that the suit would divide 4–4. Furthermore, all chance of a squeeze would be destroyed if the opponents played a second diamond. So Issie decided on another plan that did not involve a squeeze. But first it was necessary to test the clubs, just to make certain that they really were 5–3. A heart to dummy's ace and a fourth club ruff left this position:

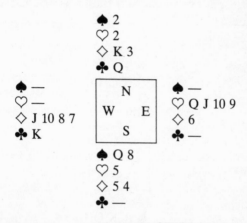

♠ 2
♡ 2
◇ K 3
♣ Q

♠ —
♡ —
◇ J 10 8 7
♣ K

♠ —
♡ Q J 10 9
◇ 6
♣ —

♠ Q 8
♡ 5
◇ 5 4
♣ —

Now a diamond to dummy's king and a heart return effectively cooked East's goose. He had to concede a ruff and discard, and that was Issie's twelfth trick.

THE LAST SAY

There is an old saying—or if there isn't there should be—that if you have x tricks on top then x+1 will usually be possible. This is particularly true of small slams with eleven on top and adequate controls. The twelfth trick can usually be made to emerge from one of the many little hidey-holes that abound in a bridge hand. Issie really played above his normal handicap mark in recognizing that any plans for a squeeze would almost certainly be thwarted by the opposition's destroying the vital diamond link. He also did well to find an alternative plan, although in fact both endings require East to hold not more than a doubleton diamond.

It would be a strange competition indeed if Aunt Agatha failed to have her occasional success. An unlucky event it may have been, but it was not all one-way traffic, as we shall see on the following hand:

Game all   (Mildred)
Dealer East   ♠ 5 3
                  ♡ K Q 10 9 4
                  ◇ 9 5 2
                  ♣ 9 7 6

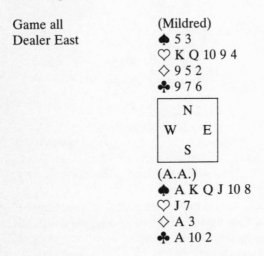

(A.A.)
♠ A K Q J 10 8
♡ J 7
◇ A 3
♣ A 10 2

Aunt Agatha virtually bludgeoned her way to 4 ♠, which does not look too happy a contract. West led the queen of diamonds. How should declarer plan the play?

Deciding that her opponents, a young pair who looked studious and alert, would never muddle their signals when it came to holding up the ace of hearts, she conceived what the industrialists call 'a viable proposition'. With only nine tricks on top and no apparent way of collecting a tenth—unless the ace of hearts was a singleton—Aunt Agatha planned that the opponents, despite their tender years, should act as Father Christmas.

This was the full hand:

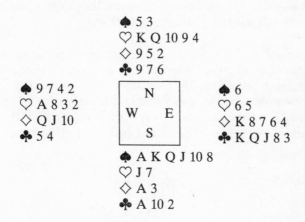

```
                    ♠ 5 3
                    ♡ K Q 10 9 4
                    ◇ 9 5 2
                    ♣ 9 7 6
    ♠ 9 7 4 2                          ♠ 6
    ♡ A 8 3 2        N                 ♡ 6 5
    ◇ Q J 10      W     E              ◇ K 8 7 6 4
    ♣ 5 4            S                 ♣ K Q J 8 3
                    ♠ A K Q J 10 8
                    ♡ J 7
                    ◇ A 3
                    ♣ A 10 2
```

The queen of diamonds was allowed to hold the first trick and the continuation won with the ace. Trumps were drawn in four rounds, dummy discarding a heart and a club. Now South exited with the two of clubs. East won and continued the suit, declarer taking her ace. A heart to dummy, West having no option but to duck, allowed Aunt Agatha to complete the key play of ruffing a diamond. Now when she produced her second heart, West was well and truly cast in the unwanted role of benefactor. Stripped of his safe cards of exit, West's only option was to duck or win the ace of hearts. In either case Aunt Agatha had her Christmas present.

THE LAST SAY

If nothing else, this hand illustrates that it is always worth searching for a plausible line of play no matter how daunting the prospects may be. Aunt Agatha could have been wrong to give up the chance of the lone ace of hearts, but the strip play, once she had thought of it, was the better bet.

Listening to Aunt Agatha describing Issie's handling of the following deal left me in some doubt as to whether she wanted him disqualified, knighted or certified. Perhaps it was all three. Anyway this was the layout that caused Aunt Agatha's blood pressure to rise so steeply. The hand occurred in the last session, when Aunt Agatha and Issie were playing the same way.

North–South game
Dealer West

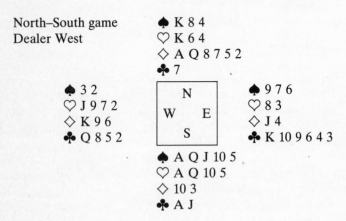

```
                  ♠ K 8 4
                  ♡ K 6 4
                  ◇ A Q 8 7 5 2
                  ♣ 7
        ♠ 3 2          N          ♠ 9 7 6
        ♡ J 9 7 2                 ♡ 8 3
        ◇ K 9 6    W       E      ◇ J 4
        ♣ Q 8 5 2      S          ♣ K 10 9 6 4 3
                  ♠ A Q J 10 5
                  ♡ A Q 10 5
                  ◇ 10 3
                  ♣ A J
```

At Aunt Agatha's table the bidding proceeded along rational lines:

S	N
(A.A.)	(Mildred)
—	1 ◇
2 ♠	3 ◇
3 ♡	4 ♣
6 ♠	

At Issie's table the bidding went the same way up to 3 ♡, then Sally bid only 3 ♠. Issie launched out into the Old Black, subsequently settling for 6NT.

Aunt Agatha had no real problems. She and her partner had bid accurately enough, and when the diamond suit behaved kindly all thirteen tricks were landed in comfort.

Issie, however, was under pressure at trick one when the two of clubs was led. East played the king, and all Issie could see for sure were five spades, three hearts, one diamond and one club—a total of ten tricks. Two more if the diamond finesse was right and the knave of hearts fell. But what worried Issie most was that if the king of diamonds was with West then all those pairs playing in 6 ♠ would almost certainly make thirteen tricks. Furthermore, if East held the king of diamonds 6 ♠ would still make but the notrump slam would be pretty remote.

Issie, therefore, came to two dynamic conclusions: (1) West, for declarer's purposes, definitely held the king of diamonds; (2) he was going to play for the jackpot, since if he went off a bottom could only be a bottom. So Issie won the first trick with the ace of clubs and immediately finessed the diamond. He then cashed the ace of hearts and ran off the spade winners. This was the position before the last spade was led:

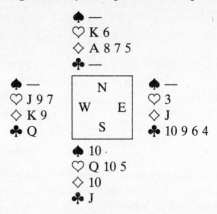

♠ —
♡ K 6
◇ A 8 7 5
♣ —

♠ —   ♠ —
♡ J 9 7   ♡ 3
◇ K 9   ◇ J
♣ Q   ♣ 10 9 6 4

♠ 10
♡ Q 10 5
◇ 10
♣ J

When the ten of spades was played West was in dire straits, eventually deciding that his best chance was to throw the queen of clubs. Of course it didn't matter what he did because Issie had only to throw a diamond from dummy and play on whichever suit West chose for his discard. On the knave of clubs, West, desperately hoping that his partner might hold the knave and ten of diamonds, threw the nine of diamonds. The rest was plain sailing.

When Aunt Agatha saw Issie's result on the travelling scoresheet (+1,470) and stopped to consider just what was needed for thirteen tricks to materialize in notrumps, she made no attempt to conceal her disgust.

'That Issie has the luck of the devil,' she exclaimed with real feeling. 'He bids so badly yet invariably emerges unscathed. It's uncanny for anyone to lead such a charmed existence.'

When confronted with the Aunt Agatha attack, Issie, trying hard to keep a straight face, retorted, 'Oh, I don't know about the devil's luck, but knavery without luck is the worst trade in the world, they tell me!'

THE LAST SAY

It has been suggested, perhaps rather unkindly, that bad bidders need to be fantastic dummy players in order to extricate themselves from the mess they get into during the auction. Be that as it may, full marks to Issie for realizing that if he was going to come out of the hand without egg on his face then he had to make at least as many tricks as those playing in the more rational contract of 6 ♠.

This sort of thinking is often needed at pairs in order to turn near disaster into resounding success. Perhaps the commonest case is where a pair reach 3NT, or at any rate a notrump contract, and then realize that they have missed their 4–4 fit in one of the majors. Ten tricks are obviously available in the major, but nine appear the limit in notrumps. Now is the time to stand on your head to try and achieve the extra trick in your notrump contract. Providing you think that most pairs will bid and make game (ten tricks) in the major, then quite extraordinary risks may be justified in order to attain parity in notrumps.

In concluding this chapter on Aunt Agatha and computerized deals, two thoughts strike me. One, like sex, whether you believe it is a good idea or not, I think the computer has also come to stay. Two, looking on the bright side, it adds a new dimension to a bridge player's list of excuses for doing poorly. While previously one had to rely on such hardy annuals as partner, bad luck, excessive noise, fixed by old ladies, fixed by young ladies, just fixed, a draught at the back of one's neck, a blonde in a miniskirt, anything in a miniskirt, and then again partner, dear partner—one can now add Frankenstein the computer.

5

The Commodore's Cup

'I shall have to enter for the Commodore's Cup you know, Mildred,' announced Aunt Agatha. 'He expects me to win it.' The uninitiated might be forgiven for thinking that the competition to which my aunt referred was an individual event. In fact, it was not even for pairs, but for teams of four. Still, little things like numbers never have bothered my aunt. The other three players were a tiresome necessity that would no doubt hinder her progress, but they were needed to complete the quorum. The Commodore was an old friend (an old flame, according to Issie). In any case he clearly knew my aunt well, for there was also no suggestion from him of a team effort. He expected *her* to win, which, if nothing else, proves that he was reared in true Aunt Agatha tradition.

The small matter of organizing a team was quickly settled. A 'royal decree' was proclaimed which required Issie, Sally and Mildred to accompany Aunt Agatha to the starting-gate on D-day. Issie, Sally and Mildred duly appeared without demur. What else? Actually Sally, who never says very much, did ask rhetorically, 'Why do we always get involved?'

'Committed, don't you mean?' enquired Issie.

'What's the difference? It seems all the same to me.'

'I'll tell you,' replied Issie, obviously delighted at getting the chance to trot out one of his famous aphorisms. 'It's like eggs and bacon. The chicken's involved, the pig's committed.' Issie's fourth-form humour is usually infectious and the others laughed appreciatively. And so to the match.

It wasn't long before Aunt Agatha was in the spotlight, facing a tricky problem on this hand.

Game all   ♠ 5 3
Dealer South   ♡ K 10 6
                   ◇ J 7 4
                   ♣ K 6 5 4 2

                   ♠ K Q J 10 9 7
                   ♡ Q 9 5
                   ◇ A K 5
                   ♣ A

The bidding:

S	W	N	E
(A.A.)		(Mildred)	
2 ♠	No	2NT	No
3 ♠	No	4 ♠	No
No	No		

West led the knave of clubs, East playing the three. Trick two
went to West's ace of spades, and when he returned the suit
Aunt Agatha drew trumps, West throwing the two of hearts on
the third round. How should declarer continue?

At the opposite table, where the contract and the play to the
first three tricks were the same, declarer continued with the
queen of hearts. No one wanted this trick, but the heart
continuation—small to dummy's ten—was taken by East's
knave. East then cashed the ace of hearts and exited with a
fourth heart. Eventually the defence had to make the queen of
diamonds. One down.

Before we see how Aunt Agatha played, perhaps we should
look at the full hand. Even then the winning line might escape
you.

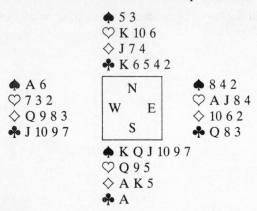

♠ 5 3
♥ K 10 6
♦ J 7 4
♣ K 6 5 4 2

♠ A 6
♥ 7 3 2
♦ Q 9 8 3
♣ J 10 9 7

♠ 8 4 2
♥ A J 8 4
♦ 10 6 2
♣ Q 8 3

♠ K Q J 10 9 7
♥ Q 9 5
♦ A K 5
♣ A

With nine tricks on top (5 spades, 1 heart, 2 diamonds and 1 club) Aunt Agatha could make one extra trick if only she could reach dummy. And there was in fact a foolproof way there (alternatively East would have to concede *two* heart tricks which would do just as well): run the nine of hearts at trick four. That is exactly what she did. East *had* to win and did his best by returning a diamond, but declarer won and led the queen of hearts, which was overtaken by dummy's king. This play left the defence without further resource.

THE LAST SAY

As it happens 3NT would have presented little difficulty, and this was a contract reached at some tables. Nevertheless, full marks to Aunt Agatha, who showed fine technique and fully deserved her game swing.

Aunt Agatha showed considerable enterprise on the next hand.

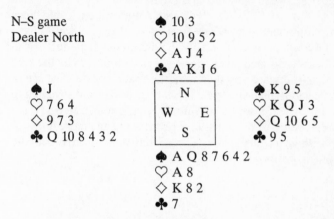

N–S game
Dealer North

♠ 10 3
♡ 10 9 5 2
♢ A J 4
♣ A K J 6

♠ J
♡ 7 6 4
♢ 9 7 3
♣ Q 10 8 4 3 2

♠ K 9 5
♡ K Q J 3
♢ Q 10 6 5
♣ 9 5

♠ A Q 8 7 6 4 2
♡ A 8
♢ K 8 2
♣ 7

Against Issie and Sally the North–South bidding was 1 ♣–
1 ♠; 1NT–4 ♠. The seven of hearts was led. Declarer won,
discarded a heart on the second top club and took the spade
finesse. East had to make one spade trick and eventually also
made his queen of diamonds. Plus 650 was a score that made
everyone happy. Issie and Sally could do no better, and the
North–South pair preened themselves on avoiding the slam
with, as they put it, 'everything wrong'.

'Everything wrong' was of course a considerable distortion of
the facts. The king of spades was well placed and so too was the
queen of clubs. It's true that the spades did not break evenly
and that the queen of diamonds was wrong, but that looks like a
fair division of good and bad.

At Aunt Agatha's table the bidding went 1NT–6 ♠. The fact
that two aces could have been missing didn't seem to bother her
and, as she explained later out of Mildred's hearing, 'The
alternative was to bid 4 ♣' (Gerber, asking for aces) 'but
imagine the catastrophe that would have been. My partner has
to reply 4 ♠, showing her two aces, and then the slam would be

played the wrong way up.' The wrong way up in Aunt Agatha language is when partner plays the hand!

The four of clubs was led, and Aunt Agatha could have finessed immediately, when most of her troubles would have been over, but understandably she did not want all her eggs in one basket. So she played the ace of clubs followed by the king for a heart discard and then took the spade finesse. The ace of spades and a small spade came next. East won and switched to the king of hearts, and now Aunt Agatha demonstrated how the contract could be made without resorting to any more finesses. She cashed all her spade winners but one, to arrive at the following position:

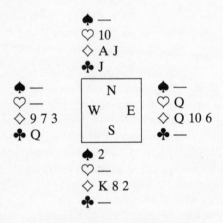

When the two of spades was played West had to retain the queen of clubs, so he threw a diamond. The knave of clubs, having done its work, was thrown from dummy and now it was East's turn to feel the pressure. He had to retain the queen of hearts so he also threw a diamond. The ace, king and a third diamond completed the success story.

THE LAST SAY

It is interesting to note the lengths to which some players will go in order to try and play the hand. Aunt Agatha even visualized the possibility of Mildred's having to respond 4 ♠ to Gerber, so she carefully bid the slam without checking on aces. According to my aunt, 'This was the lesser risk.' There might be two aces missing, but at least Aunt Agatha would be at the wheel. I really can't see what was wrong with 3 ♠, followed by 4NT over North's 3NT rebid. Maybe Aunt Agatha visualized another opportunity for a muddle over the Blackwood-or-quantitative dilemma. However, I think most players have got this clear in their minds today. After a force, 4NT *is* Blackwood.

There is another line of play, unsuccessful in the event, which must offer almost as good odds as Aunt Agatha's choice. Win the ♣ A and cash the ♣ K, discarding a heart as before. Now enter the South hand with the ♡ A and take the diamond finesse. If that wins, lay down the ♠ A to guard against a blank king with West. If the diamond finesse loses, declarer must play for trumps to be K x onside. Still, who wants to argue with success?

Aunt Agatha was not too pleased with her partner on the next hand.

Love all   ♠ A J 5 2
Dealer East   ♡ A 8 7 5 2
                   ◇ 6
                   ♣ J 10 9

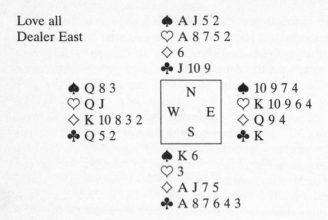

♠ Q 8 3   ♠ 10 9 7 4
♡ Q J   ♡ K 10 9 6 4
◇ K 10 8 3 2   ◇ Q 9 4
♣ Q 5 2   ♣ K

                   ♠ K 6
                   ♡ 3
                   ◇ A J 7 5
                   ♣ A 8 7 6 4 3

This was the bidding:

S	W	N	E
(A.A.)		(Mildred)	
—	—	—	No
1 ♣	No	1 ♡	No
2 ♣	No	3 ♣	No
No	No		

The queen of hearts was led, and as the dummy appeared on the table it was obvious that Aunt Agatha was far from satisfied. She didn't actually say anything, but her looks spoke volumes. Mildred, knowing the signs only too well, shifted uncomfortably on her seat. Had she bid too much? Or too little? Three clubs looked about right to her, but obviously something was wrong. Aunt Agatha soon demonstrated what it was. She won in dummy with the ace of hearts, played a diamond to the ace and ruffed a diamond. A heart ruff and a diamond ruff were followed by the ace and king of spades, and now the knave of diamonds was ruffed with dummy's last trump and overruffed by East with the king. East continued the heart suit, and Aunt Agatha ruffed with the six of clubs, West declining the overruff. However, it didn't matter as declarer now played the ace and seven of trumps. All she lost were the king and queen of trumps.

'Five notrumps cold, five clubs cold, and we have to play in a miserable part-score,' muttered Aunt Agatha, only just audibly.

'I couldn't do any more, dear,' observed Mildred, still not sure what it was that Aunt Agatha had expected of her. 'I only had ten points, you know.'

Maybe Aunt Agatha knew she was on doubtful ground for she refused to be drawn further and called for the new board. However, as it happened, Issie and Sally, with a little bit of help from the declarer, more than redressed the balance when the board arrived at their table. This was the bidding:

S	W	N	E
	(Issie)		(Sally)
—	—	—	No
1 ♣	1 ♢	1 ♡	No
2 ♣	No	2 ♠	No
2NT	No	3 ♣	No
5 ♣	No	No	No

The queen of hearts was led, and the play followed along similar lines to the first table. However, there was a small difference: the declarer omitted to cash the ace of spades, so at the point of East's overruff of the knave of diamonds this was the position:

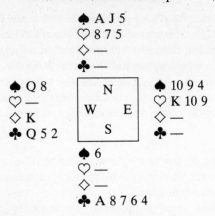

Sally led the king of hearts, declarer ruffed with the six of clubs and Issie threw the eight of spades. The declarer could still have succeeded had he cashed his ace of spades, ruffed a heart with the seven of trumps and exited with a small trump. Instead he cashed the ace of clubs and followed with the eight of clubs, which Issie gobbled up with his queen to leave this position:

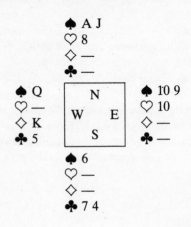

It is not often that you see the five of trumps promoted to master rank, but this was what happened when Issie played the queen of spades. Declarer's carelessness in not cashing off the ace of spades was now only too apparent, as he could not escape from the dummy without effecting the promotion. Issie was very pleased with his coup, not fully realizing at the time that South should have avoided presenting him with such a golden opportunity.

'You never would have had that chance against me,' snorted Aunt Agatha, no doubt trying to squash the ebullient Issie and at the same time draw a veil over her own indifferent contract. Besides, it was Aunt Agatha who won matches, not her team-mates, and she resented them claiming the limelight.

THE LAST SAY

Although 3NT is likely to make, despite the meagre holding of only 22 points, it is not easy to get there. Five clubs, however, looks a more realistic proposition. Perhaps Aunt Agatha should have made one effort over 3 ♣. It is unlike her to hold back in the bidding, especially when she is going to play the hand herself. Having limited her hand with 2 ♣, 3 ◇ over 3 ♣ does not look excessive. Even Mildred would then continue with 3 ♠, and suddenly the two hands can be seen to fit exceptionally well. Knowing Aunt Agatha, it would have taken no further encouragement for her to leap to 5 ♣. Perhaps the important factor to note in the bidding of this hand is that it's not just the points that each player has that matter—it's where they are, what they are, and how the two hands weld together.

As to the play at Issie's table, South forgot a cardinal rule of crossruffing: cash your side-winners first. One usually does this to prevent the defenders discarding and then trumping one's winners. However, as we have seen, it is also important on some occasions to prevent a trump promotion. At the point where South ruffed the king of hearts with the six of clubs, he should have known that it was perfectly safe to cash the king of spades. West was counted for five diamonds, two hearts and not more than three clubs; therefore he had to have a third spade.

Although one or two minor setbacks occurred after this fine start Aunt Agatha's team combined well together to rake in more points on the following hand, but it was Aunt Agatha and Mildred who took the major honours.

N–S game
Dealer West

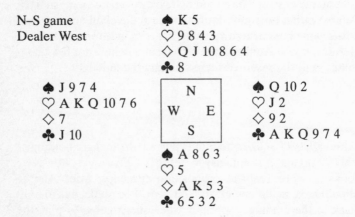

♠ K 5
♡ 9 8 4 3
♢ Q J 10 8 6 4
♣ 8

♠ J 9 7 4
♡ A K Q 10 7 6
♢ 7
♣ J 10

♠ Q 10 2
♡ J 2
♢ 9 2
♣ A K Q 9 7 4

♠ A 8 6 3
♡ 5
♢ A K 5 3
♣ 6 5 3 2

The bidding at Issie's table was effective, but slightly reminiscent of the blunderbuss:

S	W	N	E
	(Issie)		(Sally)
—	1 ♡	No	2 ♣
No	4 ♡	No	No
No			

North led the queen of diamonds which South overtook with the king and tried to cash his ace. Issie ruffed and quickly wrapped up the remainder of the tricks for a score of +480.

At Aunt Agatha's table the bidding was very different:

S	W	N	E
(A.A.)		(Mildred)	
—	1 ♡	No	2 ♣
Dble	2 ♡	4 ◇	4 ♡
No	No	5 ◇	Dble
No	No	No	

Mildred's final bid was only made after much heart-searching, a recap of the auction and several recounts of her points. No wonder East doubled. Mildred looked like a woman planning her own funeral.

Rather strangely, perhaps, East led the knave of hearts. West won and switched to the knave of clubs, followed by the ten. Mildred ruffed in hand and quickly set about ruffing her losing hearts in dummy. She had little trouble in making eleven tricks for a score of 750. So that was +15 imps to Aunt Agatha on the board.

'Was I right to carry on to five diamonds, dear?' enquired Mildred rather needlessly.

Aunt Agatha permitted herself a little smile. After all, she could afford it. The question was typical of Mildred, although many players cast in her mould come out with equally senseless queries in similar circumstances. All they really want is a pat on the back, and I am certain they are quite oblivious of the needling effect it can have on the opposition as they are busy licking their wounds. It would have been churlish of Aunt Agatha to refuse Mildred her accolade, and Mildred looked as though she could purr when Aunt Agatha replied, 'You judged it to perfection, my dear. Absolute perfection.'

When Aunt Agatha showed me the hand she said, 'Of course, neither side judged it to *absolute perfection* since both contracts can be defeated, but I couldn't tell Mildred that and spoil her moment of glory. Four hearts goes down on a spade ruff, and five diamonds fails on a trump lead and continuation when East regains the lead with a top club.'

THE LAST SAY

Aunt Agatha's analysis was a trifle hasty. It's true that Issie's four hearts could have been defeated on a spade ruff, and had North been given the chance he *might* have switched to the king of spades at trick two. Against Mildred, however, a trump lead would not necessarily have beaten the contract. Certainly it would have prevented her ruffing three heart losers in the dummy, but it would not have stopped her from putting plan B into operation. Only two hearts are ruffed in the dummy and then the play is projected to the following position with North to lead, needing the remainder of the tricks:

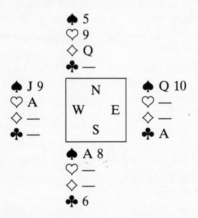

When the queen of diamonds is played the opposition are caught in a simultaneous double squeeze. East has to retain the ace of clubs, so lets go a spade. The six of clubs is now discarded from dummy, and it's West's turn to feel the pinch. He can't part with the ace of hearts, so he too has to relinquish a spade. Dummy's eight of spades takes the last trick.

There are two further points I should like to make. In competitive situations it is often right to bid one more, since it is not always easy to find 100% defence even if the contract is defeatable. Equally, the opposition are in the same position, so that 'unmakable' contracts are sometimes allowed to slip home.*

The other point concerns the bidding. Against Issie and Sally, South was unenterprising in failing to bid. It was probably going to be then or never, and the opportunity was too good to miss. Although many players worry about a shortage of points—especially at adverse vulnerability—an impeccable shape is usually more than adequate compensation. North–South combined have only 17 points, but there is no denying that the hand belongs to them. Issie's jump to 4 ♡ was exaggerated, although in the event it made life easy for Sally. Maybe this was a case of making the wrong bid at the right time: had he rebid 2 ♡, East would have had an awkward decision: 2 ♠, 3 ♣, 3 ♡ or 4 ♡? Nothing looks right. Two spades is cheap, but dangerous if West can support them (and of course he would do just that). Maybe 3 ♡ is the middle-of-the-road choice, and for that reason best.

The next hand was really a question of judgement all round. Aunt Agatha was not very sympathetic to poor Issie, who had to contend with what he called 'an obscene bidding sequence'. This was the deal.

*See also p. 139 where this point is emphasized again.

Game all

Dealer North

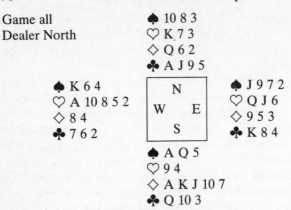

♠ 10 8 3
♡ K 7 3
◇ Q 6 2
♣ A J 9 5

♠ K 6 4
♡ A 10 8 5 2
◇ 8 4
♣ 7 6 2

♠ J 9 7 2
♡ Q J 6
◇ 9 5 3
♣ K 8 4

♠ A Q 5
♡ 9 4
◇ A K J 10 7
♣ Q 10 3

These were the two sequences:

Table 1

S	W (Issie)	N	E (Sally)
—	—	No	No
1 ◇	No	2 ♣	No
3 ◇	No	4 ◇	No
5 ◇	No	No	No

Table 2

S (A.A.)	W	N (Mildred)	E
—	—	No	No
1 ◇	No	2 ♣	No
3NT	No	No	No

Judging that he should try to develop some early tricks in spades, Issie led the four of spades against five diamonds. This was not a classic success. Declarer won with the queen, drew trumps and took the club finesse. With the ace of hearts right and the five of spades disappearing on the long club, the declarer lost just one club and one heart.

Against Aunt Agatha, in 3NT, the five of hearts was led, and it looks as though she has an almost impossible task. Five diamonds, one heart and two black suit aces total only eight tricks, and both finesses are wrong. But wait . . . East took the first trick with the knave of hearts and returned the queen, dummy's king being allowed to win. In order to find out more about the hand, Aunt Agatha ran her five diamond tricks, West discarding two clubs and a spade, North two spades and East the eight of clubs and two of spades. The picture was far from crystal clear, but if everyone was to be believed East held the king of clubs and West, perhaps, the king of spades. Working on this basis, Aunt Agatha produced the queen of clubs with a flourish (just testing), and then went up with dummy's ace. Now the seven of hearts threw West on lead to enjoy his three hearts—and lead away from the ♠ K 6. Three notrumps just made for a flat board.

'Just as well you've got me at the wheel to compensate for your dotty leads,' was my aunt's comment when she found that five diamonds had made.

Issie insisted that his lead was not so bad on the bidding, and then added, somewhat petulantly, 'If the opposition are incapable of making normal bids one has to guess, and even you, Agatha dear, might get some of them wrong.'

Agatha dear wasn't looking as though she was going to get anything wrong, and she seemed about to tell Issie so. But she thought better of it, and suggested they got back to their tables.

THE LAST SAY

This is a difficult hand to bid with any degree of accuracy. Perhaps 3NT by North is best; but whatever the contract, and whoever plays it, some luck will be needed. I think the best beginning is 1 ◇–2 ♣; 2 ♠, and now North will bid notrumps first. Without a heart stop North would find some other bid, leaving the options open. However, Aunt Agatha works on the basis that if she plays the hand it's worth several tricks to her side, and frankly it is difficult to argue otherwise.

As the play went Aunt Agatha took a bright view of the distribution, but I must emphasize that the plan she adopted would be unlikely to work against top-class opposition. Any real expert in the West seat would automatically blank the king of spades with his first two discards. Lesser lights always feel nervous of this manoeuvre, feeling sure that they will subsequently lose their king. In practice this seldom happens, as the declarer cannot *see* what has taken place and will normally continue with his own plan of finesse or end-play. Either way the perceptive defender will gain. It is also important to work out what you need to keep early on so that you don't signal your difficulties as the pressure mounts. The moment East shows an odd number of diamonds (the 3 first followed by the 5) West knows that he must find three discards, and it is at this point that he should decide on two spades and one club, *not* one spade and two clubs.

At half-time Aunt Agatha's team had taken a respectable lead, but looking at the successful quartet some of those in hot pursuit might have been forgiven for thinking that such a four would never hold their place. However, Aunt Agatha does not concede ground too easily, and no one is more aware than she how important it is to consolidate an initial advantage and prevent the gains from slipping away—hence her pep talk to the team.

'Now I don't want anyone to start relaxing just because we are a few points in front,' she said sternly. 'Try to avoid being sloppy and giving away the points that I shall unquestionably bring in.' The funny thing is that my aunt meant every word she said, and, oddly enough, her team didn't seem to resent her remarks. Not outwardly, anyway. Issie and Sally exchanged knowing glances, Mildred looked at the floor and Issie seemed about to add some profound contribution when the team were peremptorily dismissed. 'Right, back to work then, everybody. Come along, Mildred.'

As if to prove her very words a hand soon arrived on the table which required all Aunt Agatha's ingenuity—and a little help from her opponents.

Game all
Dealer North

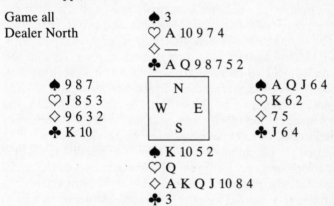

♠ 3
♡ A 10 9 7 4
♢ —
♣ A Q 9 8 7 5 2

♠ 9 8 7
♡ J 8 5 3
♢ 9 6 3 2
♣ K 10

♠ A Q J 6 4
♡ K 6 2
♢ 7 5
♣ J 6 4

♠ K 10 5 2
♡ Q
♢ A K Q J 10 8 4
♣ 3

This was the bidding:

Table 1

S	W (Issie)	N	E (Sally)
—	—	1 ♣	1 ♠
3 ♢	No	3 ♡	No
3NT	No	4 ♣	No
5 ♢	No	No	No

Table 2

S (A.A.)	W	N (Mildred)	E
—	—	1 ♣	1 ♠
3 ♢	No	3 ♡	No
4 ♢	No	4 ♡	No
4NT	No	5 ♡	No
6NT	No	No	No

At table 1 Issie led a spade to the ace, and Sally, after much deliberation, made the fine return of the king of hearts. This immediately placed the contract in peril but, with the aid of the club finesse, the declarer eventually mustered eleven tricks (seven diamonds, one spade, one heart and two clubs).

It was at table 2, however, that most of the drama took place. The bidding had an uneasy ring about it. Aunt Agatha had intended 4NT to be natural since no suit had been agreed. Indeed, there was every indication of a total misfit. But Mildred stoically stuck to her guns. Aunt Agatha had forced and subsequently bid 4NT, and that in Mildred's book was Blackwood. (I can't imagine there being any grey areas in Mildred's book. Simply a case of you do or you don't, it is or it isn't, with little or no room for self-expression.) Aunt Agatha's final bid was probably made more out of frustration than anything else. She did consider for a moment whether to bid 6 $\diamond$ or 6NT, but apparently the possibility of a spade ruff influenced her final choice.

The nine of spades was led against 6NT and won by the ace. Time stood still as East considered the position. Obviously the queen of spades continuation was safe, or a diamond switch, but, superficially at least, a club was unattractive. That left the heart suit. While a heart had much to commend it, East was afraid that Aunt Agatha might hold Q x, and that would be fatal. So—yes, it was the queen of spades. But if you think Aunt Agatha's problems are over just try making the rest of the tricks. She is in her own hand with the king of spades and this is the position:

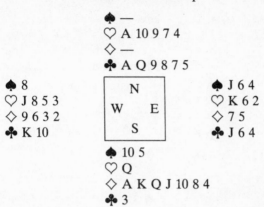

♠ —
♡ A 10 9 7 4
♢ —
♣ A Q 9 8 7 5

♠ 8
♡ J 8 5 3
♢ 9 6 3 2
♣ K 10

♠ J 6 4
♡ K 6 2
♢ 7 5
♣ J 6 4

♠ 10 5
♡ Q
♢ A K Q J 10 8 4
♣ 3

The first point to strike my aunt was that the king of clubs *had* to be right, otherwise there was no chance. But even with West holding the king of clubs there were only eleven tricks: seven diamonds, one spade, one heart and two clubs. Perhaps pressure could be brought on East in some way so that he had to relinquish one of his controls. He must hold the knave of spades, and very likely the king of hearts if West was to be given the king of clubs. If he had length in clubs as well that would be a hefty burden to bear. 'Let's see what happens,' mused my aunt playing the cards in her mind's eye. 'I play off all my diamonds except one to reach this position:

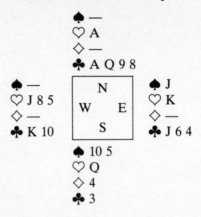

'Now when I play my last diamond, dummy throwing a club, East parts with the king of hearts and I'm doomed. Even if I keep one more heart in dummy and one less club I'm no better off.'

And then the penny dropped. The suspicion of a smile crossed Aunt Agatha's lips and suddenly she started to play off her diamonds as though there was no tomorrow. In the five-card ending above she couldn't wait to get the four of diamonds on the table and discard—not the eight of clubs, but the ace of hearts! When she called for this card Mildred looked at her in horror.

'Did . . . did you say the ace of hearts, dear?' stammered Mildred, unable to believe her ears.

'Yes, the *ace of hearts*,' replied Aunt Agatha firmly, noting with great satisfaction that East did not seem to want to make a discard. Eventually East parted with the king of hearts, only for Aunt Agatha to slap the queen of hearts on the table and once more await East's pleasure. This time the four of clubs was discarded, and Aunt Agatha took the last three clubs with the aid of the finesse.

'I never thought you would make that contract,' said East,

still slightly mystified by everything that had happened. But if East was mystified, Mildred was more so.

'Wouldn't it have been easier to have kept the ace of hearts?' she enquired.

'Not easier, impossible,' replied Aunt Agatha enigmatically. She enjoyed being the centre of a mystery, and it was far too pleasurable to elaborate further and spoil the aura of mystique.

THE LAST SAY

Shapely misfitting hands are always difficult to bid, and despite Aunt Agatha's great coup it usually pays to aim for a modest target. Five diamonds looks about right, although even this contract is no certainty, especially if East finds Sally's inspired switch to the king of hearts.

Clearly the bidding at table 2 went off the rails. Aunt Agatha started well by rebidding her diamonds, but I think 4NT was a mistake for two reasons: (1) These hands are usually best played in suits and can turn out a disaster in notrumps (best defence holds declarer to nine tricks). (2) Although many partnerships would play 4NT as a non-Blackwood bid in the quoted sequence, it was £50 to a pinch of snuff that Mildred would take it as asking for aces. As to Aunt Agatha's final choice of 6NT, rather than 6 $\diamond$, I think this was poorly judged. The chance of a spade ruff was minimal, but the odds on the hand proving unmanageable in notrumps were very short indeed. In fact if East returns the king of hearts, which locks the declarer in dummy, or a club which has the same effect, 6NT will go well down. Even if East plays the knave of spades on the first trick, declarer can come to no more than eleven tricks. However, full marks to Aunt Agatha in the play. When given a chance, although the odds must have looked insurmountable, she tackled her problem like a champion. The unblock of the ace of hearts created a triple squeeze against East, a most imaginative play and the only one to succeed.

As the Commodore's Cup gradually drew towards its climax Aunt Agatha's team suffered several jolts. Issie and Sally bid a good slam depending on one of two finesses, both wrong. At Aunt Agatha's table the East–West pair were satisfied to bid game. Then Mildred went down doubled in 4 ♡, with 3NT on ice and duly made at the opposite table. With one board to play it must have been touch and go as to who had the lead when the cards fell like this.

N–S game
Dealer North

♠ A 5
♡ K Q J 9
◇ A 7 3 2
♣ J 4 2

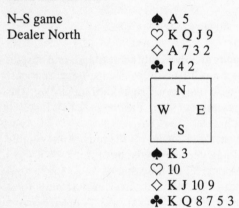

♠ K 3
♡ 10
◇ K J 10 9
♣ K Q 8 7 5 3

This was the bidding at Aunt Agatha's table:

S	W	N	E
(A.A.)		(Mildred)	
—	—	1 ♡	1 ♠
2 ♣	No	2 ◇	No
2 ♠	Dble	Rdble	No
3NT	Dble	No	No
Rdble	No	No	No

An aggressive sequence, especially South's redouble. Still, for someone playing as well as Aunt Agatha who can blame her for wielding the big axe? She may occasionally have offended the purists, but whenever she was in the driving seat the points kept rolling in with great regularity. As Issie put it some days later when the dust of battle had settled, 'Incredibly, she seemed to manufacture points like a sausage machine.'

Back to this final deal, 3NT redoubled. West leads the two of spades. Remember, the Commodore's Cup probably depends on the outcome of this hand. How should declarer plan the play?

Aunt Agatha's analysis was very sharp. If she guessed the position of the queen of diamonds she could always make three hearts, two spades and four diamonds, but if she misguessed—disaster! If she established the clubs there wouldn't be time to play on hearts, but providing the clubs were no worse than 3–1 she would make five clubs, two spades and two diamonds. The only danger to the contract then was if the clubs were 4–0. Having directed her mind to the critical factor—the club break—she realized that if East held all the clubs the suit could be picked up without loss, apart from the ace. But if West had them the suit would have to be abandoned, the ace of hearts knocked out and the queen of diamonds located. Putting plan A into operation meant that the first spade had to be won in the South hand so that a small club could be led *towards the knave*.

Time to look at the full hand:

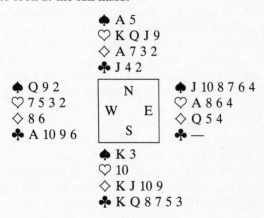

```
                ♠ A 5
                ♡ K Q J 9
                ♢ A 7 3 2
                ♣ J 4 2
   ♠ Q 9 2        ┌─────────┐    ♠ J 10 8 7 6 4
   ♡ 7 5 3 2      │    N    │    ♡ A 8 6 4
   ♢ 8 6          │ W     E │    ♢ Q 5 4
   ♣ A 10 9 6     │    S    │    ♣ —
                  └─────────┘
                ♠ K 3
                ♡ 10
                ♢ K J 10 9
                ♣ K Q 8 7 5 3
```

West had to allow dummy's knave of clubs to win trick two, East discarding a heart, and already it was time for plan B (knock out the ace of hearts and guess the position of the queen of diamonds). East took the king of hearts and cleared the spades, West unblocking the queen. Three rounds of hearts followed, East discarding a spade and South three clubs. Aunt Agatha now paused to take stock. East had presumably started with six spades to the J 10, the ace to four hearts and, since he had a club void, three diamonds. West therefore had queen to three spades, four small hearts, a doubleton diamond and ace, ten, nine to four clubs. But who had the queen of diamonds? Going over the bidding didn't really help. East could have bid 1 ♠ without it, while an aggressive West might have bid as he did with a spade fit and the club suit bottled up—regardless of his holding in diamonds. So Aunt Agatha decided to rely on the odds. With three diamonds in the East hand and only two in the West it was 3–2 in favour of East holding the queen. Without more ado she played the ace of diamonds, then low to the knave and cashed the king and ten. Ten tricks made for a score of 1,350.

What a way to finish a competition, especially as Issie and Sally had collected 100 points at their table, where the contract was 3NT by North. Sally (East) led a spade. The declarer won with the ace and played a low club towards the length in dummy. When East showed out there was no way to recover.

Aunt Agatha made only a flimsy pretence at concealing her pleasure over the result of this last hand, while her left-hand opponent was quite incapable of disguising his disgust. There is certainly something about redoubled contracts that gets the adrenalin going at top speed.

'Damned lucky!' muttered West. 'If I hold the queen of diamonds they lose 1,000 points—1,000 points, what a swing!'

'Of course we were lucky,' retorted Aunt Agatha. 'Lucky that the clubs didn't break and lucky with our opponents, too.'

'What's that supposed to mean?' enquired the sourpuss on Aunt Agatha's left. Oh my, what an unwise question.

'Well, if the clubs break any idiot could make 3NT, so there would probably be no swing, and with less aggressive opponents I don't get the chance to redouble and teach them a sharp lesson.' Touché!

THE LAST SAY

This was an awkward deal that needed careful and precise handling. West's double could be labelled 'lunatic' or 'brilliant' according to one's mood. Where one suit is going to behave badly and you have a fit with partner it is surprising how often the whole hand is in danger of collapse. Against that the partnership can be—and indeed is—woefully short of points. There is no reason for it to be otherwise, but perhaps West was unlucky to meet Aunt Agatha at this particular moment.

Note Aunt Agatha's careful analysis, essential at all times but especially so when the stakes are high, as in slams and doubled and redoubled contracts. First she saw that she could make the contract by playing on hearts and guessing the diamonds correctly. Not wanting to guess unless it was essential, she turned her attention to clubs. Here it was a question of the break; with 2–2 or 3–1, nine tricks were certain, but there would be no time to play on hearts. And then the 64-dollar question: how would she be affected if there were four clubs in one hand? This may sound like a lot to consider at the table, involving a lengthy pause before playing a card, but I'm sure most experts would cover the ground quite quickly and less-experienced players can soon develop the technique.

'If you two have just kept your heads, I think I've won it,' announced Aunt Agatha as Issie and Sally rejoined their table.

'We've played a great game,' replied Issie refusing to be outdone by Aunt Agatha now that the contest was over. 'I think we've won it too,' he added with a smile.

'What's that minus 100 I see on board 26?' enquired Aunt

Agatha glancing at Issie's card. 'They bid 4 ♠ and make five against us. It was a lay-down.'

'Atrocious bidding. Sally and I bid to six, a contract that depended on one of two finesses. A wonderful slam.'

'You need to have a feel for these things, Issie dear,' replied Aunt Agatha illogically, and then, anxious to get away from this hand, which she now recalled was a 76% slam, 'Come along, let's get on with the scoring.'

At the final count Aunt Agatha's team had eight points to spare over their nearest rivals, so the last hand had done it.

Aunt Agatha still recalls her triumphs in this match and often refers to the time '*I* won the Commodore's Cup'. Oddly enough, the others, including Issie, now accept this claim with good grace, for there was no doubt that Aunt Agatha really excelled herself. A glittering star in a cloudy sky she may well have been. Even so I think the mousy Mildred deserves a word of praise. She did nothing exceptional, but then she did nothing that was really bad either, and that is often how matches are won. Furthermore, to play with a straight bat when facing my aunt is no mean achievement—but please don't tell Aunt Agatha I said so!

6

Aunt Agatha Plays
Multiple Teams

The very name of the game, 'Teams', tends to suggest a gathering of people pulling together in the same direction with the same objective. All for one and one for all. A laudable concept, no doubt, but Aunt Agatha is far too much of an individualist to fit so neatly into the theoretical pigeon-hole.

On her day she will carry the rest of the team, almost regardless of what they do, but invariably those who make up the supporting cast are subjected to a great deal of criticism, especially when the burden has proved too great! Inevitably bridge players make mistakes, or at least take wrong views, which is when Aunt Agatha is inclined to wield the lash. Whether criticism ever is justified must be extremely doubtful, but the law of justification has never been Aunt Agatha's brightest guiding star.

Whenever Aunt Agatha finishes a losing session of bridge one can take it for granted that her partner has played poorly. And if it is a team event, the other pair had better watch out! Praise and admiration for the other half of the alliance is about as probable as similar tributes in a contested divorce case. Brickbats don't just fly through the air, they zoom around the arena with the speed and efficiency of a supersonic jet.

After a certain multiple teams event I got myself cornered by my aunt, who had a great tale of woe to unburden on me.

'Just look at this hand, Freddie. I played my usual immaculate game and what happened?'

'Tell me,' I replied, recognizing my cue—or so I thought.

'I was about to when you interrupted,' snapped my aunt.

'Those moronic idiots masquerading under the pseudonym of team-mates were given every opportunity to shine but, of course, they muddled the defence.'

This was the hand that caused the current outburst:

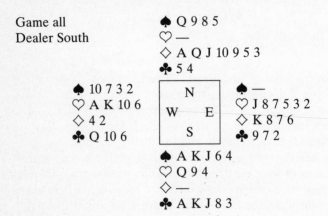

Game all
Dealer South

♠ Q 9 8 5
♡ —
♢ A Q J 10 9 5 3
♣ 5 4

♠ 10 7 3 2
♡ A K 10 6
♢ 4 2
♣ Q 10 6

N
W   E
S

♠ —
♡ J 8 7 5 3 2
♢ K 8 7 6
♣ 9 7 2

♠ A K J 6 4
♡ Q 9 4
♢ —
♣ A K J 8 3

The popular contract was 6 ♠ by South, and the opening lead was the ace of hearts.

Aunt Agatha's team-mates, defending as East-West, maintained that there was nothing they could have done to break the slam. Declarer ruffed the heart lead in dummy, played the ace of diamonds and then the queen. East covered with the king—it would not have helped him to duck—and South ruffed with the four of spades. Now the ace of spades was followed by the six of spades to dummy's nine, and diamonds were continued. West was able to ruff when he liked, but after that declarer was in control, drawing the last trump with dummy's queen of spades. Simple enough.

At Aunt Agatha's table, where she was South also in 6 ♠, the play went the same way to the first three tricks, except that Aunt Agatha ruffed the king of diamonds with the ace of spades. Now the king of spades disclosed the bad trump break, but Aunt Agatha was in complete control as she played the four of spades to dummy's nine and continued in a manner similar to that of her counterpart at the opposite table.

So there was no swing on the board, but have you absorbed the difference in technique and considered the ramifications of that difference? Aunt Agatha could not go down, but her opposite number was on less firm ground. This was the position after the first four tricks:

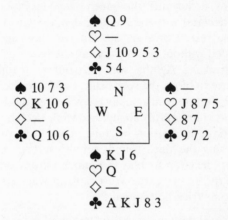

When the six of spades was played towards the dummy, West, who knew the exact position, should have inserted the ten of spades. That would have created a whole new ball game.

'They play in a complete dream, you know,' complained my aunt. 'Goodness knows what they think about. It certainly isn't bridge, and I doubt very much if it's sex. That narrows the field a bit . . .'

Aunt Agatha maintained an absolutely straight face as she looked at me for sympathy but I believe that, deep inside, her inner woman was having a quiet laugh with herself. This is not the first time I have noticed a sort of Jekyll-and-Hyde reaction which I believe Aunt Agatha thoroughly enjoys—but never shares.

THE LAST SAY

This is a strange deal in several different ways. Looking at all four hands one can see that thirteen tricks are frigid. Declarer ruffs the heart lead in dummy, discards a heart on the ace of diamonds, plays a club to the ace and ruffs his last heart. The king of clubs, a club ruff, the queen of spades and a diamond ruff leaves declarer with the simple task of drawing trumps and claiming the rest. However, that line of play can hardly be recommended without peering into all the hands.

Although Aunt Agatha was particularly scathing about West's failure to block the spade suit, I am sure she must have noticed that declarer can actually recover from this body-blow. Diamonds are temporarily abandoned while declarer falls back on the favourable division in clubs. Three rounds of clubs, dummy ruffing the third round, set the suit up and it only remains for declarer to play a diamond from dummy and discard the queen of hearts. West can ruff when he likes, but that is the only trick he can make.

While I was still thinking about the last hand Aunt Agatha was busy recording another horror story.

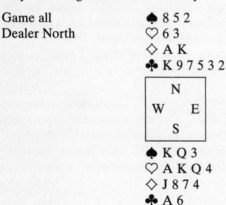

Game all   ♠ 8 5 2
Dealer North   ♡ 6 3
    ◇ A K
    ♣ K 9 7 5 3 2

```
        N
    W       E
        S
```

    ♠ K Q 3
    ♡ A K Q 4
    ◇ J 8 7 4
    ♣ A 6

With the opposition silent throughout, South becomes the declarer in 3NT. West leads the six of spades, East contributing the ten. How should South plan the play?

Maybe your reactions would be similar to those of Issie.

'Not much of a problem here,' he said to himself. 'Looks like a Momma-Poppa spread.'

Well, is it a Momma-Poppa spread? Here is the full hand:

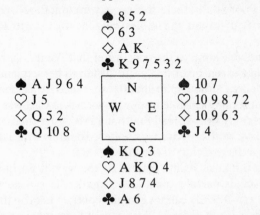

Issie won the opening lead with the king of spades and played the ace, king and another club. Now there was nothing to stop him making eleven tricks. Easy enough—as the cards lie. But suppose East has three clubs and West two? Now it would be necessary to play low on the first round of spades. From that moment onwards declarer's troubles are over.

At the tables where South decided to refuse the first round of spades, the suit was continued by East. West won the second round and knocked out declarer's last guard, East discarding the two of hearts. A critical situation now arose with regard to the play of the club suit. Some declarers carelessly played the ace, king and another, thereby meeting the fate they deserved—one down—while others cashed the ace and then played a low club from both hands. East won with his knave, but the contract was now safe.

Aunt Agatha's other pair, playing North–South, had gone down by ducking the spade and then playing off three rounds of clubs. To redeem the situation Aunt Agatha, defending as West, had to be really wide awake. Play followed the popular pattern. Three rounds of spades, then the ace and another club. It was at this point that Aunt Agatha showed a real touch of class: instead of contributing the ten of clubs she played the queen! Poor South, there was no way for him to recover. Aunt Agatha had turned the tables very neatly . . . to level the board.

Before you jump to the conclusion that Aunt Agatha's play was either eccentric or lucky, just listen to her explanation.

'My play, although brilliantly reasoned, was completely clear-cut for any sensible bridge player, since East was marked with precisely ♣ J x. Had South held ♣ A J x then he would surely have won the first spade, entered dummy with a diamond and played a low club to the knave.'

Good thinking, Aunt Agatha. By the way, if East has a less perspicacious partner than Aunt Agatha he can do his own nursing act. It really cannot give the contract to drop the knave of clubs under the ace . . . just in case West makes a mistake. Maybe Aunt Agatha does not need nursing, but if your partners are anything like mine then nursing is a full-time job.

THE LAST SAY

Well, should South duck that first spade? As the cards lie, the answer, of course, is 'No'. But as a straightforward basic principle of probabilities, if a certain defender is known to be long in one suit (it is fair to presume that West has led from length in spades) then he is less likely than his partner to hold the greater length in any other given suit. Add to this the possibility that South may more easily be able to duck a club to East than to West, and you have a clear-cut play. 'Yes', South should duck that first round of spades.

Note Aunt Agatha's reasoning for going in with the queen of clubs on the second round of the suit—a kind of crocodile coup (the jaws open and swallow up East's high card). The reasoning is impeccable and illustrates the sort of question a thoughtful defender should ask himself. Questions under the heading 'Why didn't the dog bark?' are often just as pertinent as 'Why is he doing that?'

'I find it particularly aggravating to save cheaply against a lay-down slam and then discover that "they" have muddled it.'

Aunt Agatha was off again, and this time I made no comment as I waited for the inevitable diagram.

Love all
Dealer South

♠ K Q 9 5
♡ A 7 6
♢ A Q
♣ A 8 6 4

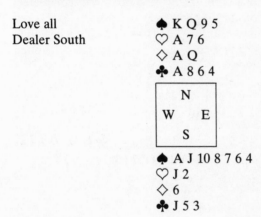

♠ A J 10 8 7 6 4
♡ J 2
♢ 6
♣ J 5 3

The bidding:

S	W	N	E
3 ♠	4 ♢	4NT	5 ♢
No	No	6 ♠	No
No	No		

West led the five of hearts, which was won in dummy with the ace, East contributing the four. Declarer then entered her own hand with a trump, both opponents following, in order to take the diamond finesse. With that hurdle successfully negotiated, she cashed the ace of diamonds, shedding her heart loser, and ruffed a heart, East following with the nine and West the three. Dummy was now entered with a trump, West discarding a low diamond and East the seven of clubs, and a second heart was ruffed, East following with the queen and West with the eight, to leave declarer with one remaining task. How should she play the club suit so as to lose not more than one trick? If you have made up your mind let us look at the full deal:

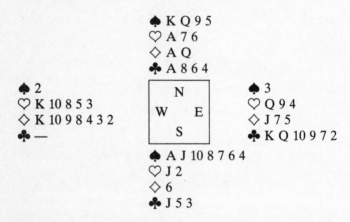

```
                    ♠ K Q 9 5
                    ♡ A 7 6
                    ◇ A Q
                    ♣ A 8 6 4
    ♠ 2                             ♠ 3
    ♡ K 10 8 5 3        N          ♡ Q 9 4
    ◇ K 10 9 8 4 3 2  W   E        ◇ J 7 5
    ♣ —                 S          ♣ K Q 10 9 7 2
                    ♠ A J 10 8 7 6 4
                    ♡ J 2
                    ◇ 6
                    ♣ J 5 3
```

Before continuing the saga of what happened in 6 ♠, let us see how they got on at Aunt Agatha's table where she sat West. The bidding was the same up to 6 ♠, but then Aunt Agatha pressed on to 7 ◇ which, naturally enough, was doubled. As the bits and pieces fell into place Aunt Agatha felt completely satisfied with her result—the loss of a mere 700.

'Cheap against the *cold* slam,' she insisted to anyone who would listen.

Meantime, back to Aunt Agatha's team-mates, North–South

at the opposite table. South was having her problems. She could not make her mind up as to the best method of tackling the clubs. This was the position with South to lead:

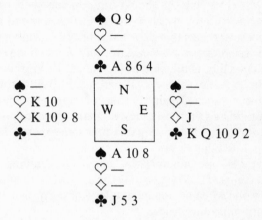

♠ Q 9
♡ —
◇ —
♣ A 8 6 4

♠ —
♡ K 10
◇ K 10 9 8
♣ —

N
W   E
S

♠ —
♡ —
◇ J
♣ K Q 10 9 2

♠ A 10 8
♡ —
◇ —
♣ J 5 3

In practice she led a low club towards dummy and when West showed out there was no recovery. Minus 50, instead of plus 980, was a bitter pill to swallow. Of course, my aunt's description of this slam as 'lay-down' was a typical piece of hyperbole. Nevertheless, I think South should have come up with the right answer.

THE LAST SAY

One can argue away about declarer's problem *ad infinitum*, but the crux of the matter is simply this: is it more likely that West has a void or a doubleton in clubs? Remembering that West chose to bid diamonds at the four level, not hearts, and apparently has heart length, a void seems the more probable answer. Furthermore, this view is endorsed by East's discard of the seven of clubs on the second round of spades, and indeed the cards played to the red suits, plus of course the bidding.

One need not concern oneself with a singleton honour, or the doubleton K Q with East, since both legitimate methods of play would succeed. If declarer thinks that West is unlikely to hold more than one club she should enter dummy with a spade and lead a low club towards her knave. East is now end-played.

If declarer thinks that West has a doubleton club, then a club to the ace is correct. Now declarer will have to hope that one of those two clubs is the king or the queen. If West unblocks his honour, the knave of clubs will become the twelfth trick. And if he doesn't, a second round of clubs will force a ruff and discard. This would be a pretty ending, but all the evidence points to the first solution and Aunt Agatha had some reason for feeling disappointed that South did not find it.

There is one minor point about the bidding. Regular partnerships should agree how best to treat their replies to Blackwood when an opponent intervenes. My own preference is both simple and logical:

With no ace: double (this must be the most disappointing hand you can have for partner).

With one ace: pass (a good moment not to increase the level).

With two aces: bid one suit up.

With three aces: bid two suits up.

It is hard to sympathize with Aunt Agatha when she is on her high horse, hating the world in general and bridge players in particular, but it did seem that the gods were not entirely on her side. Most of her good plays had come to naught and even those protagonists of a more equable temperament might have shown some strain in similar circumstances.

'It's not that I expect them to play as well as I do,' complained my aunt, 'but it would be nice to have team-mates and partners demonstrate that they are sometimes on my side.'

The next hand was, as Aunt Agatha put it, 'the final nail in the coffin'.

Aunt Agatha sat East, and these were the North–South cards:

North–South game
Dealer East

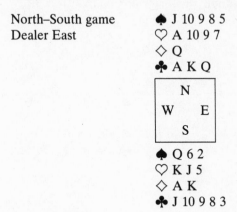

♠ J 10 9 8 5
♡ A 10 9 7
◇ Q
♣ A K Q

♠ Q 6 2
♡ K J 5
◇ A K
♣ J 10 9 8 3

The bidding:

S	W	N	E
—	—	—	No
1 ♣	No	1 ♠	No
1NT*	No	3 ♣	No
3NT	No	4NT	No
No	No		

*15–16 points

The auction was sound enough: 3 ♣ was, of course, forcing, and 4NT quantitative. South, who was minimum for his rebid, had nothing further to add.

West led the four of diamonds. At trick two declarer led the knave of hearts, West contributing the two and East the six. So far South had every reason to feel pleased with himself, and the thought of a fine score for the inevitable eleven tricks was no doubt gratifying. Do you agree with that assessment?

A glance at the full deal will show that Aunt Agatha had done some pretty shrewd thinking. She realized that there was more to be gained by ducking the knave of hearts than by taking it, so she had played low without the suspicion of a tremor.

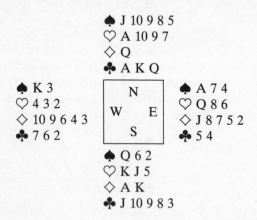

With the air of a man who only has to tidy up the loose ends, declarer started to cash his club winners, returning to hand with the king of hearts. This was the position after the first seven tricks:

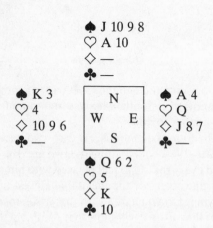

Declarer has won all the tricks so far, seven of them, and has three more on top, but if he is to enjoy the favourable heart position (!) the likely plan will be this: cash the minor-suit winners and then take the 'marked' heart finesse . . . but if that is how the play goes, Aunt Agatha will win the queen of hearts and the defence will take the next three tricks. One down!

Right on course for the minefield, declarer cashed the ten of clubs and the king of diamonds. But wait a moment. We haven't observed West's discard on the ten of clubs. Aunt Agatha had a diamond all ready but West was still huddling. Eventually the four of hearts appeared on the table, and that was the end of a beautiful partnership! The cat was out of the bag. On the five of hearts South called for dummy's ace and looked mighty relieved as he realized what had happened.

Aunt Agatha has never been the same woman since that day.

THE LAST SAY

Opportunities for the sort of coup that Aunt Agatha was trying to bring off are rare, but if the intended victim can be lured into the trap when the stage is set, and partner has the nous not to give the show away, the rewards are usually handsome. In this instance the cost to Aunt Agatha's side was unlikely to be more than 1 imp while the gain might well have been 13 imps.

Perhaps Aunt Agatha's ploy is more easily recognizable in this sort of situation:

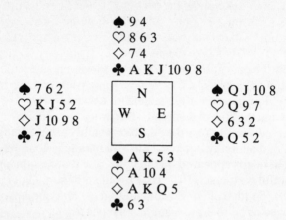

♠ 9 4
♡ 8 6 3
◇ 7 4
♣ A K J 10 9 8

♠ 7 6 2
♡ K J 5 2
◇ J 10 9 8
♣ 7 4

N
W   E
S

♠ Q J 10 8
♡ Q 9 7
◇ 6 3 2
♣ Q 5 2

♠ A K 5 3
♡ A 10 4
◇ A K Q 5
♣ 6 3

South plays in 3NT, and West decides to make the safe lead of the knave of diamonds rather than lead away from his heart tenace. South wins and plays a club to dummy's knave, West following with the seven. If East allows the finesse to succeed, South may be tempted into playing for the jackpot. In fact a repeat finesse, which would be necessary to bring in the complete suit in the event of West holding the Q 7 5 4, would result in a two-trick set. East may consider the risk of ducking justified, since the reward is so highly attractive. But if he is going in for this sort of coup he must do his thinking in advance, so that no clues are provided at the time the suit is played.

7

The Pewter Cup

In competition for the Pewter Cup, the local team-of-four championship, it was the old firm again. A reluctant Mildred partnering Aunt Agatha, with Issie and Sally making up the four. Mildred had tried to back out of it but Aunt Agatha was not accepting no for an answer and bullying tactics eventually won the day. Much the same can be said of Issie and Sally, who were certainly not falling over themselves to complete the team, but, as had happened so often in the past, they eventually succumbed.

Issie had taken one or two wrong views early on, which didn't please Aunt Agatha, and was inclined to blame it on his biorhythms, which pleased her even less.

'My biorhythms are all at a low ebb and my emotional cycle is at a critical stage. That's why I can't seem to make a single right guess,' complained Issie.

'What utter nonsense!' retorted Aunt Agatha. 'I've heard of some weird excuses for palpably poor play, but blaming it on your biorhythms is ludicrous. I suppose you'll tell us next that your stars are adversely affected by Mars, or some such mumbo-jumbo.'

'Just because you don't understand these matters there is no reason to pour scorn on them,' replied Issie huffily.

'Well, at least I understood how to play this hand,' announced Aunt Agatha, with a degree of finality in her tone. For the moment all discussion of biorhythms, lucky stars and the like ended as the players looked again at the following hand:

Love all   ♠ A K 6
Dealer East   ♡ K 5
                            ◇ A Q 10 7 5
                            ♣ A Q 2

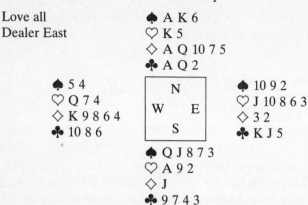

♠ 5 4   ♠ 10 9 2
♡ Q 7 4   ♡ J 10 8 6 3
◇ K 9 8 6 4   ◇ 3 2
♣ 10 8 6   ♣ K J 5

                            ♠ Q J 8 7 3
                            ♡ A 9 2
                            ◇ J
                            ♣ 9 7 4 3

Although the final contract was the same in both rooms, the bidding had taken different routes. At Issie's table North had opened 2 ♣, and eventually South pressed on to 6 ♠. In Aunt Agatha's room it was Mildred who finally took the plunge after a more conservative opening. This was their sequence:

S	W	N	E
(A.A.)		(Mildred)	
—	—	—	No
No	No	2NT	No
3 ♠	No	4 ♣	No
4 ♡	No	5 ◇	No
5 ♠	No	6 ♠	No
No	No		

Returning to the first table, Issie (West) led a trump to declarer's queen. South now ran the knave of diamonds, which was allowed to win; indeed, it would have been fatal for Issie to cover, but whatever his decision the rest of the hand looked simple enough. Were there not five spades, two hearts and a ruff, three diamonds and one club? A total of twelve tricks. Proceeding on this basis declarer cashed the top hearts, ruffed a

heart and then played off the ace of spades and ace of
diamonds to leave this position:

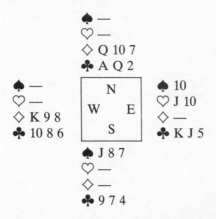

It was dummy to play and suddenly a new picture had
emerged. It was going to be an uphill struggle after all, and
maybe that king of clubs would have to be favourably placed.
Anyway, the queen of diamonds was led from dummy, East
electing to throw a heart and South a club. West won with the
king of diamonds and switched to a club, and now South had
another decision to make. Should he finesse the club, or hop up
with the ace and discard his last club on the ten of diamonds,
hoping that West had the ten of spades? He opted for the latter
plan—not that it mattered—but East killed all further prospects
when she produced the missing trump. One down, and +50 to
East–West.

At Aunt Agatha's table, West decided to lead a crafty eight
of diamonds. After some thought Aunt Agatha ran the
diamond to her knave and then, giving up all possibility of a
heart ruff, she drew trumps ending in dummy. The ace and
queen of diamonds followed, East discarding a heart and South
two clubs. In with the king of diamonds, West switched to the
ten of clubs. Aunt Agatha won in dummy with the ace, cashed

the ten of diamonds, throwing her last club, and ruffed the two of clubs. This was the position:

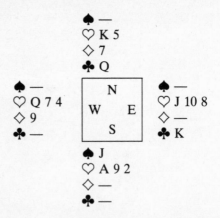

When the knave of spades was played West had to let go a heart, otherwise dummy's seven of diamonds would become good. Having done its work, the diamond was discarded from dummy, and now it was East's turn to feel the pinch. He also had to part with a heart in order to retain the master club. Out of sheer devilment Aunt Agatha led the *nine* of hearts to dummy's king, played the five back to her ace and—with mock astonishment—claimed her twelfth trick with the two of hearts.

Mildred was full of admiration for Aunt Agatha's play. Anyone who could produce the two of a side suit for the twelfth trick must be some sort of genius, she reckoned. No doubt it is only moments like this that hold a rather shaky partnership together.

THE LAST SAY

Aunt Agatha certainly read the cards well. Rejecting the club finesse in favour of the double squeeze was quite masterly. She would have been wrong had West held the king of clubs, but apparently East had momentarily tranced over Mildred's 4 ♣ cue-bid. That tell-tale sign was just enough to convince Aunt Agatha that the club finesse was wrong. Perhaps a more resourceful East, realizing the way the auction was heading, would have doubled 4 ♣ thus making sure that his partner got away to the killing lead. As the bidding went, even if West had noticed the slight trance (and not everyone is as alert as Aunt Agatha), he might have felt ethically inhibited from leading a club. But he had a second opportunity to shine when in with the king of diamonds. At this point he should have led a heart which effectively breaks up the double squeeze. A club switch is only correct when West holds the king of clubs since it provides declarer with an immediate losing option.

Issie didn't have to work too hard to score points on the next hand.

North–South game   ♠ K J 9 6
Dealer West   ♡ 3 2
                       ♢ A 9 4 2
                       ♣ A K Q

♠ A Q 10 8 3
♡ A Q
♢ K 5 3
♣ 9 5 3

This was the bidding in Issie's room:

S	W	N	E
	(Issie)		(Sally)
—	3 ♡	Dble	No
6 ♠	No	No	No

Issie led the knave of diamonds. Declarer won in hand, drew trumps in two rounds and cashed the top clubs, West showing a doubleton and then discarding the knave of hearts. How would you continue?

Here is the full hand:

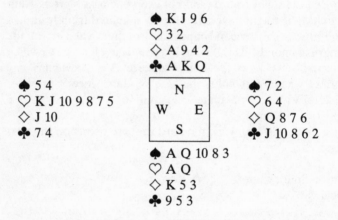

In practice declarer played the ace and another diamond, but when this suit failed to break he had to go one down, losing one diamond and one heart.

Aunt Agatha was quick to point out that declarer could have made his contract quite easily. Draw trumps, cash the minor-suit winners and then play the ace and queen of hearts. West must now concede a ruff and discard for the twelfth trick.

In Aunt Agatha's room the bidding was also over quickly but not everyone would approve of her somewhat unilateral choice:

S	W	N	E
(A.A.)		(Mildred)	
—	3 ♡	Dble	No
6NT	No	No	No

'I had to bid notrumps to protect my heart holding,' explained Aunt Agatha somewhat illogically. Perhaps on firmer ground she continued, 'Besides, it made sure I would be declarer.'

Again West led the knave of diamonds, and Aunt Agatha won with the king. Two rounds of clubs were followed by two rounds of spades, leaving this position with South to play:

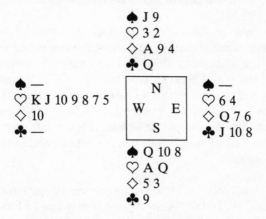

```
                    ♠ J 9
                    ♡ 3 2
                    ◇ A 9 4
                    ♣ Q
    ♠ —                           ♠ —
    ♡ K J 10 9 8 7 5      N       ♡ 6 4
    ◇ 10              W       E   ◇ Q 7 6
    ♣ —                  S       ♣ J 10 8
                    ♠ Q 10 8
                    ♡ A Q
                    ◇ 5 3
                    ♣ 9
```

Aunt Agatha now played a diamond towards dummy, and when West followed with the ten she ducked. It did not help East to overtake and leave the nine of diamonds good in dummy, so West was left on lead but he then had to play into Aunt Agatha's heart tenace. So that was +1,440 to Aunt Agatha, and a swing of 19 imps on the board.

Aunt Agatha was very pleased with herself over this success and pointed out to anyone who would listen how necessary it was for her to play only two rounds of each black suit—reading the distribution exactly—so as to prevent West from ditching the ten of diamonds.

THE LAST SAY

In fact Aunt Agatha's analysis was not quite right. True, she must not cash more than two clubs immediately, but there is nothing to stop her cashing her spades. If West then discards the ten of diamonds, East becomes a marked man. If he retains all his diamonds, the ace of hearts and ace of clubs are cashed, and he is then end-played in diamonds. Alternatively, if he discards a diamond, then the fourth diamond can be established in dummy.

Let's go back to the contract of 6 ♠ in Room 1. Aunt Agatha's suggestion of cashing the side-suit winners and then playing the ace and queen of hearts works perfectly well, but would have failed had West's shape been 2–6–3–2. Assuming that West would be unlikely to lead the knave of diamonds from J x, it seems that a small diamond towards the A 9 4 is more likely to gain than the end-play in hearts. This way you succeed when the distribution is as it was, and also when West has any three diamonds.

On the next hand Mildred incurred her partner's displeasure in no uncertain way. In fact, Aunt Agatha nearly burst a blood-vessel as she contemplated the deal later on. Mildred is now occupying the South seat.

Love all
Dealer South

♠ 10 9 4
♡ 3
♢ A K J 10 5
♣ K J 5 3

♠ A Q J 5
♡ A Q 10
♢ 9 8 7
♣ Q 7 4

The bidding:

S	N
(Mildred)	(A.A.)
1 ♠	2 ♢
2NT	3 ♠
3NT	

West led the six of hearts to South's ten, East following with the five. How should declarer plan the play?

In fact Mildred took the diamond finesse immediately, losing to East's queen. East returned a heart to the queen and king, and West cleared the suit. Subsequently West regained the lead with the king of spades for a two-trick set (three hearts and one trick in each of the other suits).

This was the full deal:

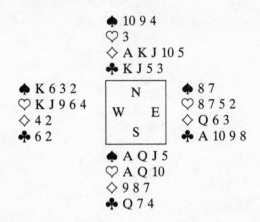

```
            ♠ 10 9 4
            ♡ 3
            ◇ A K J 10 5
            ♣ K J 5 3
♠ K 6 3 2        N        ♠ 8 7
♡ K J 9 6 4   W     E     ♡ 8 7 5 2
◇ 4 2            S        ◇ Q 6 3
♣ 6 2                     ♣ A 10 9 8
            ♠ A Q J 5
            ♡ A Q 10
            ◇ 9 8 7
            ♣ Q 7 4
```

What particularly annoyed Aunt Agatha was that they had made 3NT plus one in the other room. Issie had also led a heart, but now declarer entered dummy with a top diamond and ran the ten of spades. When it held he continued with a spade to the knave. West now took his king of spades and switched to a club, won by the ace. The hearts were cleared but declarer no longer needed the diamond finesse as he had by this time mustered three spades, three clubs, two hearts and two diamonds, a total of ten tricks.

'Why didn't you play a diamond to the ace and then attack spades?' demanded Aunt Agatha, glaring at Mildred. She should have known she was wasting her time as Mildred is very set in her ways.

'Oh no, dear,' muttered Mildred, none too confidently. 'One must attack the long suit when playing in notrumps.'

Aunt Agatha snorted and, perhaps realizing the futility of further discussion, satisfied herself with a black look all round.

THE LAST SAY

Of course, Mildred was unlucky to find everything wrong, but these are the very situations where you can make your own luck. Aunt Agatha, and South in the other room, were correct in their approach. The contract is ironclad against any distribution if declarer gives priority to the timing element. In very simple terms, East is a danger because he can play through the remaining ♡ A Q. West is no danger because if he obtains the lead he cannot attack any suit to real advantage. If the diamond finesse is wrong there are *not* nine tricks immediately available, therefore declarer must finesse first of all into the West hand.

This hand very much reminds me of one played by Jim Sharples in a Gold Cup match back in the 1960s and described by Jeremy Flint and myself in *Bridge in the Looking Glass*:

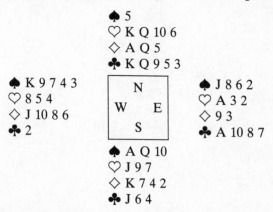

```
                    ♠ 5
                    ♡ K Q 10 6
                    ◇ A Q 5
                    ♣ K Q 9 5 3
    ♠ K 9 7 4 3    ┌─────────┐    ♠ J 8 6 2
    ♡ 8 5 4        │    N    │    ♡ A 3 2
    ◇ J 10 8 6     │  W   E  │    ◇ 9 3
    ♣ 2            │    S    │    ♣ A 10 8 7
                   └─────────┘
                    ♠ A Q 10
                    ♡ J 9 7
                    ◇ K 7 4 2
                    ♣ J 6 4
```

The contract in both rooms was 3NT by South and in each case West led the four of spades. In room 1 the declarer played a low club to dummy's king at trick two. East won and returned a spade, and now there was no way of making nine tricks before the defence took five.

In room 2 Jim Sharples, the British international, demonstrated how it should be done. He led a diamond to dummy at trick two and followed with a small club towards the knave. East had no option but to duck and now Jim turned his attention to hearts. Thus he made two spades, three hearts, three diamonds and one club.

What a pity Mildred doesn't read good books!

Poor Issie was in trouble on this next hand, but before seeing him in action you might like to consider Aunt Agatha's problem in defence:

East–West game
Dealer East

```
        (dummy)
        ♠ A 7 5 3
        ♡ A K Q J 7 5          ┌─────────┐
        ◇ 10 3                 │    N    │
        ♣ 7                    │ W     E │
                               │    S    │
                               └─────────┘
        (A.A)
        ♠ J 6 2
        ♡ 2
        ◇ A 8 7 6
        ♣ A K J 10 9
```

The bidding:

S	W	N	E
—	—	—	No
1 ♣	2 ♡	No	2 ♠
No	4 ♠	No	No
No			

You lead a top club, partner following with the two and

declarer the eight. What now? Judging that there was little hope of defeating the contract unless she found her partner with the king and another diamond, Aunt Agatha led a low diamond.

This was the full deal:

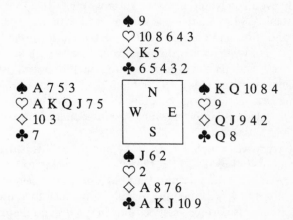

```
                    ♠ 9
                    ♡ 10 8 6 4 3
                    ◇ K 5
                    ♣ 6 5 4 3 2
 ♠ A 7 5 3          ┌─────────┐      ♠ K Q 10 8 4
 ♡ A K Q J 7 5      │    N    │      ♡ 9
 ◇ 10 3             │ W     E │      ◇ Q J 9 4 2
 ♣ 7                │    S    │      ♣ Q 8
                    └─────────┘
                    ♠ J 6 2
                    ♡ 2
                    ◇ A 8 7 6
                    ♣ A K J 10 9
```

Mildred won with the king of diamonds and after much fumbling returned a diamond to Aunt Agatha's ace. A third diamond sealed declarer's fate for there was no longer any possible route to success. East tried ruffing with the ace of spades, but when the trumps failed to break he had to admit defeat.

'What on earth were you thinking about when you won with the king of diamonds?' enquired Aunt Agatha, who had obviously suffered during Mildred's pregnant pause and incessant fumbling.

'I thought you might want a heart ruff,' replied Mildred meekly. And then, gaining confidence a little, 'After all, I could *see* eleven hearts and declarer might well have had a doubleton.'

Superficially that seemed a plausible argument, and no doubt Mildred was expecting some praise for getting her problem right. It was not, however, forthcoming. Instead, Aunt

Agatha's contemptuous rejoinder subdued Mildred into a pained silence.

'If I had wanted a heart ruff I would first have cashed my ace of diamonds and followed it with the eight. After that sequence of play even you would not have got it wrong.'

Actually, Aunt Agatha was very pleased with her result on this hand. She had played a shrewd defensive game and she knew it. However, when the time came to compare scores it transpired that they had lost 10 imps on the board, Issie's opponents having made 5 ♣ doubled.

'We can't help it if you don't bid your lay-down games,' said Issie, a little petulantly, as Aunt Agatha demanded to know what had happened.

The story was simple enough. The first three bids had been the same (No–1 ♣–2 ♡) but then North, refusing to be shut out, raised his partner's clubs. East bid 3 ♠, South passed and West raised to 4 ♠. When the bidding came back to South he decided that his partner must be short in spades and therefore bid 5 ♣. Issie's double closed the auction. Apparently Issie had cashed his major-suit aces and switched to a diamond, leaving declarer with no further problems.

As Aunt Agatha listened to the story it was obvious that she was getting more and more irritable. Almost before it had finished she fixed Issie with an icy glare and said, 'Lay-down game, my foot. Any *bridge player* sitting West would realize that four into three doesn't go, and if he had not led a trump at trick one then he would certainly switch to one after the ace of hearts. *Now* make your lay-down contract!'

Wisely, Issie did not try, but quickly drew attention to the next hand.

THE LAST SAY

Perhaps it is typical of Mildred that she did not think her hand was worth a bid at favourable vulnerability. Of course, it could

be argued that that would only have led to a contract of 5 ♣—
which can, and should, be beaten—whereas 4 ♠ cannot be
made against best defence. Maybe, but experience shows that it
is usually right to bid one more in these close competitive
situations for three good reasons:

1 They may make their contract, even though it is
   defeatable;
2 you may make your contract, even though it is defeatable;
   and
3 they may decide to bid 'one for the road', leaving you
   confident of a plus score.

The reason Issie was anxious to get on to the next board was
because he thought they must have gained a few points.

'We pushed through a thin one on this hand and I had to play
it jolly carefully,' he burbled. And then, looking at Aunt
Agatha's score-card, 'It's hardly surprising that they settled for
a part-score against you.'

For convenience Issie is now shown in the South seat. This
was the deal:

Game all   ♠ K Q 6
Dealer South   ♡ J 10 9 8
                  ◇ 5 4 3 2
                  ♣ K 2

                  ♠ J 8 5 3
                  ♡ 7
                  ◇ A K Q 9 7
                  ♣ A 9 5

The bidding, for what it is worth, went like this:

S	N
(Issie)	(Sally)
1 ◇	1 ♡
1 ♠	3 ◇
3NT	

This is a reasonable contract, despite the meagre point count, and 3NT looks an inevitable bid after Sally's jump preference to three diamonds.

West led the queen of clubs. What do you think? Did Issie have to play carefully to land the spoils?

To give Issie his due, it did not take him long to isolate the problem and, as is so often the case, once he had done that the execution of the successful plan was not too difficult. Nine tricks were there unless the diamonds divided 4–0. If West had four, then there was not much he could do about it . . . but if East held them all, that was a very different matter.

At trick one Issie made the key play of winning the club lead in his own hand. The wisdom of this move will be appreciated when you study the full deal:

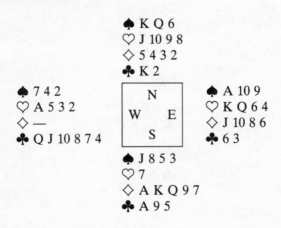

```
                    ♠ K Q 6
                    ♡ J 10 9 8
                    ◇ 5 4 3 2
                    ♣ K 2
   ♠ 7 4 2              N           ♠ A 10 9
   ♡ A 5 3 2                        ♡ K Q 6 4
   ◇ —          W           E       ◇ J 10 8 6
   ♣ Q J 10 8 7 4        S          ♣ 6 3
                    ♠ J 8 5 3
                    ♡ 7
                    ◇ A K Q 9 7
                    ♣ A 9 5
```

When West showed out on the ace of diamonds a small spade to dummy established the second entry. This enabled Issie to pick up East's diamonds without loss. Note the effect if declarer happens to win the opening lead with the king of clubs in dummy. Since the ace of spades is off side, he has no hope of recovery.

'I don't know what you're making such a song and dance about, Issie,' said Aunt Agatha ungraciously. 'It looks pretty routine stuff to me.'

'Really,' replied Issie, more like his normal self again with his biorhythms at least temporarily forgotten. 'You may not believe this but I've actually known a few pairs fail to get to 3NT when holding only twenty-three points between them. But then maybe their card-play is not so immaculate as mine,' he added, almost as an afterthought.

Aunt Agatha glared at Issie. She did not appreciate his humour, and from her point of view the conversation was getting out of hand. 'If you've quite finished blowing your own trumpet perhaps we can get on with the scoring,' she suggested icily. 'What about the next board, did you play brilliantly and defeat them in 3NT?' There was just a faint hint of sarcasm in her voice that was not missed by the others.

'They only bid two and we held them to eight tricks,' interjected Sally, anxious to avoid Issie's antagonizing Aunt Agatha again.

'Just as well I was playing this hand, otherwise we might have lost points,' continued Aunt Agatha with all her usual modesty.

Before we go on to the next hand . . .

THE LAST SAY

A word of praise for Issie. The notrump game looks ironclad, with five diamonds, two clubs and at least two spades all there for the taking. At moments like this it is always right to direct your mind to this simple question: is there anything that can go wrong? That question will inevitably lead to a closer inspection of the diamond suit and then, as the implications are grasped, to the availability of entries—and finally to a viable plan. Issie was certainly right on target.

This was the next hand that Aunt Agatha was anxious to get on with:

North–South game
Dealer West

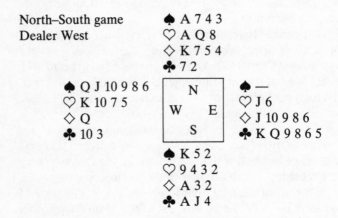

North:
♠ A 7 4 3
♡ A Q 8
◇ K 7 5 4
♣ 7 2

West:
♠ Q J 10 9 8 6
♡ K 10 7 5
◇ Q
♣ 10 3

East:
♠ —
♡ J 6
◇ J 10 9 8 6
♣ K Q 9 8 6 5

South:
♠ K 5 2
♡ 9 4 3 2
◇ A 3 2
♣ A J 4

The bidding:

S	W	N	E
(A.A.)		(Mildred)	
—	No	1 ♠	2NT
Dble	No	No	3 ♣
3NT	No	No	No

As so often happens, the 'unusual' 2NT helped Aunt Agatha with the distribution and location of the missing cards while doing nothing useful for the defence.

West led the queen of spades, which Aunt Agatha ducked, and followed with the knave, East throwing clubs. Aunt Agatha won the second trick in her own hand and played a heart to dummy's eight. East won and switched to the knave of diamonds, taken by the king. A club from dummy saw East on lead once more as he went in with the queen and Aunt Agatha ducked. The diamond continuation was also ducked (the fourth trick for the defence) and a third round of diamonds won by the ace. Now a successful heart finesse followed by the ace left this position, dummy to play:

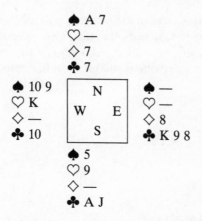

```
              ♠ A 7
              ♡ —
              ◇ 7
              ♣ 7
  ♠ 10 9   ┌─────────┐   ♠ —
  ♡ K      │    N    │   ♡ —
  ◇ —      │  W   E  │   ◇ 8
  ♣ 10     │    S    │   ♣ K 9 8
           └─────────┘
              ♠ 5
              ♡ 9
              ◇ —
              ♣ A J
```

When Aunt Agatha took the club finesse West was not yet inconvenienced, but on the ace of clubs he could not spare any of his three cards and Aunt Agatha was home. A nicely timed squeeze.

'Not bad,' conceded Issie. 'Still, it does look pretty routine stuff to me.'

THE LAST SAY

At favourable vulnerability one really can't blame East for getting active in the bidding, although I am sure it eased Aunt Agatha's burden. With only six tricks on top there is a lot of work to do. Even if it is assumed that the king of hearts is right, there are still two more tricks to find and good breaks were ruled out the moment East opened his mouth. Placing the king and queen of clubs with East (and the king of hearts with West) there is still one more vital trick to find and that *has* to come from a squeeze. Having diagnosed the symptoms, Aunt Agatha prescribed the right medicine with deadly efficiency. Lose four tricks early on, so that when the screw is turned there will be no escape.

With Aunt Agatha in such form, it will probably come as no surprise to anyone to learn that the Pewter Cup now resides on her sideboard, cherished as though it were made of gold. Furthermore, everyone is still on speaking terms.

8

I Join Aunt Agatha's Team for a Practice Match

I am a sucker, and I know it. I seem to spend half my life doing things that I have no wish to do and am always regretting that I didn't take evasive action in the first place. Which brings me to Aunt Agatha's practice match. Just what she was practising for remains something of a mystery, but there was certainly no mystery about my involvement.

'It's getting near Christmas,' said my aunt, 'the time of year when favourite nephews are nice to everyone, especially doting aunts. Besides, we need you to make up the team.'

The very thought of Aunt Agatha doting on anybody is really quite hysterical. Even with Christmas approaching, when understandably the hostile barriers may be lowered a little, it is hard to visualize Aunt Agatha actually doting. About as probable as Wedgwood Benn applying for membership of the Tory party.

Anyway, as I said, I'm a sucker and that is no doubt the reason why I found myself partnering Aunt Agatha in her match against Issie's team. Issie was playing with Mildred, but I never really discovered who all the others were, except that our team-mates answered to the names of Dottie and Percy, which was surely an inauspicious start. Not that I have anything against the Dotties and Percies of this world. Many of them may well be the salt of the earth, but somehow these names fail to ring a bell of confidence. Who ever heard of Dottie and Percy winning the championship?

It wasn't long before there was a vulnerable game swing, and I was in trouble.

North–South game
Dealer East

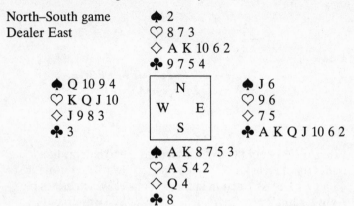

♠ 2
♡ 8 7 3
◇ A K 10 6 2
♣ 9 7 5 4

♠ Q 10 9 4
♡ K Q J 10
◇ J 9 8 3
♣ 3

♠ J 6
♡ 9 6
◇ 7 5
♣ A K Q J 10 6 2

♠ A K 8 7 5 3
♡ A 5 4 2
◇ Q 4
♣ 8

This was the bidding in our room:

S	W	N	E
(Issie)	(F.N.)	(Mildred)	(A.A.)
—	—	—	3NT
4 ♠	Dble	No	No
No			

I led the king of hearts, and Issie pondered for some time before making a move. The bidding had clearly indicated distributional storms, but paradoxically this very factor was like manna from heaven, for how could declarer succeed if the spades and diamonds divided evenly? Having absorbed this strange phenomenon—that bad breaks were not only to be expected but were actually essential for success—Issie played out his cards with rare panache. Ace of hearts, ace and king of spades, queen of diamonds and a diamond to dummy's ten. When the ten held and Aunt Agatha could not ruff the ace of diamonds Issie looked like a puppy-dog with two tails. Of course, I had to keep following suit while Issie threw a club and a heart. By the time I was able to ruff, yet another heart had disappeared, and so we collected just two spades and one heart.

'Didn't you know that I had the club suit?' enquired Aunt Agatha, furious that she had been done out of her club trick and that Issie had got home.

'Of course,' I replied, 'but the king of hearts looked the natural lead. Anyway, I'm not sure that we necessarily defeat the contract if I lead a club.'

'Rubbish!' retorted Aunt Agatha, none too graciously. 'We murder him on a club lead. In any case I like my partners to lead *my* suit. That gives *me* a better chance to direct the defence.'

'But you bid notrumps,' said Issie. 'How could Freddie lead a notrump?'

Aunt Agatha was not amused, and the withering look she gave Issie would have silenced stronger mortals.

In the other room the bidding took a slightly different course, although the final contract was the same:

S	W	N	E
—	—	—	4 ♣
4 ♠	Dble	No	No
No			

West, my opposite number, no doubt reared in the obedient traditions of Aunt Agatha, duly led the three of clubs. East won and continued clubs, South ruffing and West correctly refusing to overruff. If in fact West is tempted to overruff declarer can make his contract in the same way as Issie. As it was, South had to face the problem of West discarding a diamond. He tried the ace, king and another spade but when the suit failed to break and West switched to the king of hearts there was no way to avoid the loss of four tricks.

THE LAST SAY

In fact the second declarer, who turned out to be Percy, might have given himself a better chance. Suppose he judges that the spades are likely to be 4–2, which is probable enough on the bidding and the play to the second trick. So now he leads the ace and a *low* spade. No doubt East will win this trick, and the question arises—what should she play? If she has become sufficiently besotted with her club suit and the merits of a forcing game, the defence will fail. Declarer simply ruffs the club continuation, and if West overruffs his last trump can be drawn. If West again refuses the overruff declarer will force out the trumps by playing the king and another. Then the diamond suit plus the ace of hearts will look after the remainder of the tricks. To beat the contract East must switch to a heart after winning the knave of spades. Now declarer is left without further resource.

In many ways this is a fascinating hand, for it is fatal to play hearts early on yet equally fatal not to play them at a later stage. 'Whosoever shall master the art of timing is assuredly destined for the most succulent rewards.' I wonder who said that.

The duel on the next hand was really worthy of a more august occasion. One could well imagine the excitement of a bridgerama audience following the parry and thrust of two great teams locked in combat in some exotic championship, which perhaps only goes to show that the Aunt Agathas and Issies of this world all have their moments.

North–South game
Dealer West

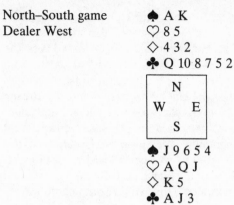

♠ A K
♡ 8 5
♢ 4 3 2
♣ Q 10 8 7 5 2

♠ J 9 6 5 4
♡ A Q J
♢ K 5
♣ A J 3

The bidding:

S	W	N	E
(Issie)	(F.N.)	(Mildred)	(A.A.)
—	No	No	No
1 ♠	No	2 ♣	No
2NT	No	3NT	No
No	No		

You might like to put yourself in the declarer's seat as we reach various stages of the play. The three of hearts is led and you take East's seven with your queen. You play a spade to dummy, West producing the queen and East the two, and lead the ten of clubs. East follows with the six and West the nine. How should you continue?

Issie had been tempted to reject the club finesse altogether, laying down the ace at trick two. However, this could have had disastrous results if East had held the king of clubs and West the ace of diamonds. That was why Issie embarked on the club finesse. At trick four Issie led a second club, East played the four, and West won with the king! West now switched to the ten of diamonds. East, Aunt Agatha, won with the ace and, right on cue, promptly knocked out dummy's spade entry, West throwing the six of diamonds. Issie now played a club to his ace which caused Aunt Agatha to give her discard some thought. Eventually she parted with the knave of diamonds, while West threw the seven of diamonds. How would South continue?

Time to look at the full hand:

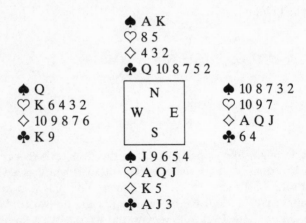

```
                 ♠ A K
                 ♡ 8 5
                 ◇ 4 3 2
                 ♣ Q 10 8 7 5 2
  ♠ Q              ┌─────────┐      ♠ 10 8 7 3 2
  ♡ K 6 4 3 2      │    N    │      ♡ 10 9 7
  ◇ 10 9 8 7 6   W │         │ E    ◇ A Q J
  ♣ K 9            │    S    │      ♣ 6 4
                 └─────────┘
                 ♠ J 9 6 5 4
                 ♡ A Q J
                 ◇ K 5
                 ♣ A J 3
```

So far it seems that the defence have been gaining all the Oscars, but Issie was not finished yet. This was the position after he had won the ace of clubs. South to play, having taken five tricks and lost two:

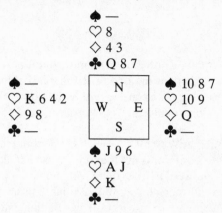

Reading the cards with commendable skill and playing right up to his top handicap mark, Issie found the only winning line when he exited with the knave of hearts. West won and returned a heart, but now Issie cashed the king of diamonds and got off lead with the six of spades. Poor Aunt Agatha was end-played and had to concede the last two tricks to a jubilant Issie.

You will notice that it would not have helped Aunt Agatha to discard a heart, rather than a diamond, on the third round of clubs. Now all Issie has to do is cash the ace of hearts and king of diamonds and exit with a low spade once more. East will make her queen of diamonds, instead of West making the king of hearts, but she will still have to concede the last two spade tricks.

In the other room Dottie and Percy sought refuge in 5 ♣ played by North. After a heart lead and spade return from West this contract stood no chance.

THE LAST SAY

Three notrumps by South looks a far more natural contract than
5 ♣ by North. Also, the major-suit attack is on balance likely to
be more rewarding than starting with a diamond, although on
this occasion a diamond lead would prove a greater embarrassment.

It may seem that West takes a big risk in ducking the club, but
in practice it seldom works out that way. West can see that if the
club suit is allowed to run there can be little prospect of
defeating the contract, so the small risk that South will drop the
king on the second round is well worth the gamble. Such
plays—dropping the honour after an apparently successful
finesse—are rarely made except when the opposition give
themselves away. If the defenders do their thinking well in
advance and hold their cards up, there is no reason to assume
that declarer will suddenly decide that he is being taken for a
ride.

Until now, without putting too fine a point on it, the match had
not gone well for Aunt Agatha. Although there had been some
gains on the smaller hands, the big fish had proved too slippery
to catch. No doubt this factor was uppermost in Aunt Agatha's
mind as she bulldozed her way through the auction on the
following hand:

North–South game
Dealer West

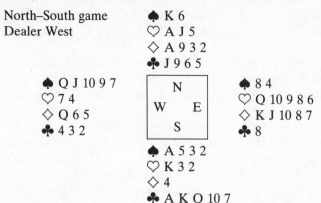

```
              ♠ K 6
              ♡ A J 5
              ◇ A 9 3 2
              ♣ J 9 6 5

♠ Q J 10 9 7      N        ♠ 8 4
♡ 7 4                      ♡ Q 10 9 8 6
◇ Q 6 5      W       E     ◇ K J 10 8 7
♣ 4 3 2           S        ♣ 8

              ♠ A 5 3 2
              ♡ K 3 2
              ◇ 4
              ♣ A K Q 10 7
```

The bidding:

S	N
(A.A.)	*(F.N.)*
—	1NT
3 ♣	3 ◇
4NT	5 ♡
5NT	6 ◇
7 ♣	

Not a great sequence, but once Aunt Agatha gets an idea into her head it takes a lot to dislodge it. She scented a grand slam right from the off, and once all the controls were located there was no stopping her. Just what would have happened had my king of spades been the king of diamonds, I really don't know. Somehow, I suspect, the blame would have been pinned on me. When I put this point to Aunt Agatha later on she replied, in her own inimitable way, 'That's the worst of you scientists and prophets of doom. You always imagine that disaster is just around the corner. You want someone to hold your hand before you venture out into the dark.'

'Oh, I don't know . . .' I began.

'Of course you don't,' interrupted Aunt Agatha. 'That's why you would do well to model your bidding on mine.' Now there's a thought!

Anyway, back to the hand. West led the queen of spades, and Aunt Agatha's main problem was how to dispose of the heart loser. Obviously, there was the heart finesse, but no good player likes to put all her eggs in this particular basket. Aunt Agatha won the spade lead in dummy and drew two rounds of trumps, East throwing the ten of hearts. Play continued with the ace of spades and a spade ruff, East discarding a diamond on the third round, followed by the ace of diamonds and a diamond ruff. East played the king of diamonds on the second round of this suit and when a spade ruff and a second diamond ruff came next, East discarded the six of hearts on the spade.

Aunt Agatha had gleaned a great deal of information by now and had fully made up her mind how to continue. This was the position:

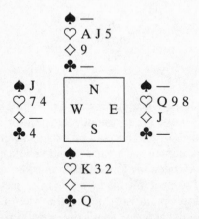

Declarer had counted West for five spades, three clubs and probably only three diamonds. So, if this were the position, East could be squeezed in the red suits. Without further ado she drew the last trump, throwing a heart from dummy. East did his best by throwing a heart, but Aunt Agatha's ace, king and three of hearts took the last three tricks.

Whatever Aunt Agatha lacked in bidding technique she certainly made up for in dummy play. Realizing early on that there was plenty of time for the heart finesse, should she wish to take it, she disposed of her spade losers while at the same time isolating the diamond control and building up a general picture of the hand. In the end position it was just possible that West had started life with four diamonds to the queen, knave and a singleton heart—which could have been the queen. However, this was not only against the odds but also inconsistent with East's early discard of a diamond—an improbable move holding six hearts and four diamonds.

Not surprisingly, the opposition only bid a small slam in the other room, so that was 13 imps to Aunt Agatha.

THE LAST SAY

I thought our auction left much to be desired. So often players tend to rush to Blackwood when a series of cue-bids would be far more illuminating. In fact all the key controls can be shown if the bidding goes like this:

S	N
—	1NT
3 ♣	3 ♢
3 ♠	4 ♡
5 ♡	5 ♠
7 ♣*	

In the play of the hand, however, Aunt Agatha earned ten out of ten and one for neatness (as my old schoolmaster seldom

*Seven clubs is still something of a gamble (the doubleton spade is fortuitous), but when one is looking for points some risks have to be taken.

used to say). Note the careful buildup of the overall picture, drawing important inferences from the discards. Pundits of the game will no doubt reflect that this feature—study the early discards (from what holding would the defender most readily have made those discards?)—was Terence Reese's Bols Tip, and in my view one of the most valuable contributions of all.

The next hand of interest was again played by Aunt Agatha, but first we'll see what happened when her opposite number played it.

Game all   ♠ K 5 3
Dealer South   ♡ K 3 2
                      ◇ K J 10 8
                      ♣ J 10 9

                      ♠ A 8
                      ♡ A Q 8 5
                      ◇ A Q 7 4
                      ♣ A 4 2

The bidding:

S	N
2NT	3 ♣*
3 ◇	4 ◇
4 ♡	4 ♠
6 ◇	

Baron—asking for suits upwards

West led the queen of spades. Mildred, who was South in the other room, won in her hand, drew trumps in three rounds and then, when the hearts failed to break, took two finesses in clubs. Contract made.

The bidding took a similar route in our room and the final contract was again 6 ◇ by South. Aunt Agatha was at the helm, and once again the queen of spades was led and won by declarer. Aunt Agatha now drew trumps, East discarding a spade on the third round, played a spade to the king and ruffed a spade, West throwing a club on the third spade. It was at this point that Aunt Agatha went into a protracted huddle. It was clear to her that if the hearts broke there would be no further problem. But as West had only five cards in spades and diamonds the 3–3 heart division did not seem likely.

There remained then the question of split honours in clubs. But what if West had both the king and queen of clubs? Aunt Agatha soon realized that there was a way of enjoying the best of both worlds. If the hearts didn't break and the club honours were split, or West had them both, she could make her contract by ruffing out the fourth heart. Then she would only lose in the event of East having started life with both the king and queen of clubs. Although the odds were fairly close, this seemed a distinctly better bet than the double finesse, especially since West almost certainly began with more clubs than his partner.

Having made a very shrewd analysis of the position, Aunt Agatha cashed the ace, king and queen of hearts, East throwing a second spade on the third round of hearts. But now, having ruffed a heart and played a club, she found that East did in fact hold both the king and queen of clubs so Aunt Agatha was one down.

This was the full deal:

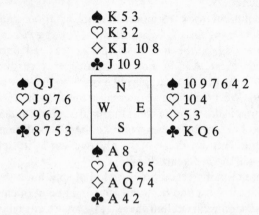

When Aunt Agatha heard what had happened when Mildred played the hand in the other room you could have cut the atmosphere with a knife.

'Why is it that morons, idiots and palookas are always so richly rewarded at this game?' she enquired, of nobody in particular. 'You know,' she continued, 'no guardian angels exercise greater diligence than those who safeguard the interests of the palookas.'

With that profound statement released for posterity we proceeded with the match, but first of all . . .

THE LAST SAY

Aunt Agatha had a difficult decision to make. Taking the straightforward double-club finesse (a 76% chance) succeeds when the king and queen are split or when East has them both. On the other hand, Aunt Agatha's line of play also succeeds when the club honours are split and when West has them both. That seems to suggest that the two lines of play offer identical chances. What perhaps swings it in Aunt Agatha's favour — although it hardly justifies her vitriolic outburst—is that before the critical decision is taken West is known to have started with four clubs against East's three. With no psychological factors to fall back on, that distinct shade of odds suggests that Aunt Agatha was right—although on this occasion unlucky.

At the half-way stage of the match Aunt Agatha's team had fallen a little behind.

'Just imagine, 29 imps behind to Issie and his cripples. It's unbelievable. Unless we pull our socks up that wretched little man will never stop crowing.'

So, carefully heeding my aunt's ominous warning, we duly ensured that our socks were wrinkle-free and back we went into battle. It wasn't long before Aunt Agatha demonstrated that bit of class for which she is rightly renowned, and this time there was no ill-fortune to dog her efforts.

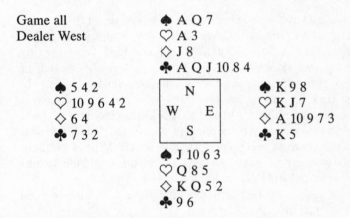

Game all
Dealer West

♠ A Q 7
♡ A 3
◇ J 8
♣ A Q J 10 8 4

♠ 5 4 2
♡ 10 9 6 4 2
◇ 6 4
♣ 7 3 2

N
W E
S

♠ K 9 8
♡ K J 7
◇ A 10 9 7 3
♣ K 5

♠ J 10 6 3
♡ Q 8 5
◇ K Q 5 2
♣ 9 6

Let's first see what happened to our team-mates, Dottie and Percy, who were North–South in the other room. They found little difficulty in making 3NT after the following auction:

S	W	N	E
—	No	1 ♣	Dble
1NT	No	3NT	No
No	No		

West led the four of hearts, dummy played low and East won with the king. After a heart return East was soon in again, when the declarer played the ace and another club. East now cleared the hearts but his side had only one more trick to take—the ace of diamonds. So that was +630 to Aunt Agatha's team.

In our room this was the bidding:

S	W	N	E
(Issie)	(F.N.)	(Mildred)	(A.A.)
—	No	1 ♣	Dble
No	1 ♡	3 ♣	No
3NT	No	No	No

A slightly different auction, but it all amounted to the same thing; well, more or less the same thing. The same contract, played the same way up against the same lead. Only one tiny factor was different: Aunt Agatha sat East. Instead of contributing the king of hearts when dummy played low to the first trick, Aunt Agatha very smoothly produced the knave. Issie won with the queen and took a losing club finesse. Aunt Agatha now returned the king of hearts and Issie's fate was sealed. There were eight tricks to take, but no hope of the ninth since we had one in the bag and were waiting to gobble up four more immediately we regained the lead.

When the dust had settled a little, Issie reluctantly agreed that he had misplayed the hand.

'Not once but twice, just for good measure,' as Aunt Agatha so pungently described it. What she meant was that Issie had three ways of playing the heart suit. His method was doomed to failure. But had he risen with the ace on the first round, or refused to play his queen on the knave, then the contract could not have been defeated. Despite Issie's careless lapse, all credit to Aunt Agatha for making the best of her chances.

THE LAST SAY

A beginner learns at an early stage 'not to finesse against partner' and therefore builds up a resistance to withholding his highest card in positions like the above. Praiseworthy though this dogma may be, there are usually exceptions to all good rules and in this case one emerges because the key word is *communication*. Once East appreciates the necessity of maintaining a link with her partner's hand, and the near certainty that West will have no outside card of entry, the play of the knave of hearts becomes marked.

South was fortunate in that he could afford to give up his second heart trick, if he so desired, since the defence had nowhere to go. This will not always be the case, as the following diagram shows:

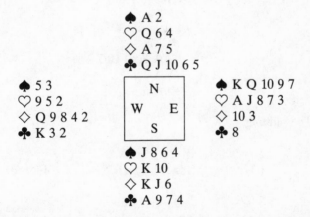

```
                    ♠ A 2
                    ♡ Q 6 4
                    ◇ A 7 5
                    ♣ Q J 10 6 5
    ♠ 5 3              ┌─────────┐      ♠ K Q 10 9 7
    ♡ 9 5 2            │    N    │      ♡ A J 8 7 3
    ◇ Q 9 8 4 2        │  W   E  │      ◇ 10 3
    ♣ K 3 2            │    S    │      ♣ 8
                       └─────────┘
                    ♠ J 8 6 4
                    ♡ K 10
                    ◇ K J 6
                    ♣ A 9 7 4
```

Suppose South becomes the declarer in 3NT after East has overcalled 1 ♠. West dutifully leads the five of spades, dummy plays low, and East . . . ? If he contributes a high honour, the declarer can always prevail by playing him for the knave of hearts. But suppose he puts in the nine of spades. South *must* win this trick but is now likely to be defeated. No doubt he will enter dummy with the ace of diamonds to take the club finesse. West wins, and with the communications still intact, he continues spades. Declarer's prospects have now plummeted to zero. Indeed, he may well try the diamond finesse as a last resort and finish two down.

It was not long before Aunt Agatha was once again demonstrating her skills, this time as declarer.

Game all
Dealer East

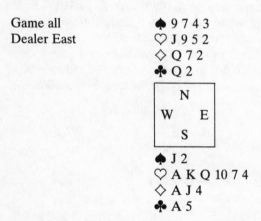

♠ 9 7 4 3
♡ J 9 5 2
♢ Q 7 2
♣ Q 2

♠ J 2
♡ A K Q 10 7 4
♢ A J 4
♣ A 5

The bidding:

S (A.A.)	W (Issie)	N (F.N.)	E (Mildred)
—	—	—	No
2 ♡	2 ♠	3 ♡	No
4 ♣	No	4 ♡	No
No	No		

When the dummy went down it was obvious that Aunt Agatha didn't think much of my raise.

'You didn't consider asking me for aces, by any chance?' she enquired sarcastically.

Determined not to be outmanoeuvred, I replied that I was anxious not to extend her unduly, but if we had missed a slam then she could blame me. A withering look shot across the table and then, no doubt satisfied that she had had—in a sense—the last word, Aunt Agatha got down to her task of trying to make the contract.

Issie led the ace of spades and then switched to the three of hearts. East followed with the eight of spades, but discarded the four of clubs on the first round of hearts. Before reading on perhaps you would like to consider what plans you would make in Aunt Agatha's position.

I am quite sure Aunt Agatha didn't fancy her chances, but whatever one may say about my aunt from time to time—and a good deal of it is unprintable—she is at heart a great trooper. Thus it came as no surprise to see her setting about her task with considerable determination.

Aunt Agatha won the heart switch in her own hand and promptly played back the knave of spades. That was a far-sighted gambit and one of the essential preliminary stepping-stones to success. West won with the queen and played a second heart, East completing a peter in both spades and clubs. This time Aunt Agatha won the heart in dummy and ruffed a spade, East discarding a small diamond. Now a third round of hearts gave dummy the lead once more enabling Aunt Agatha to ruff out the last spade, East throwing a diamond and a club. This was the full hand:

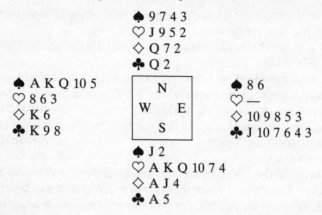

There was an uncanny hush as Aunt Agatha won her fifth trick and paused a while for further thought. Everyone seemed to sense that the most critical stage of the hand had just been reached and that a dynamic decision was about to emerge. This was the position:

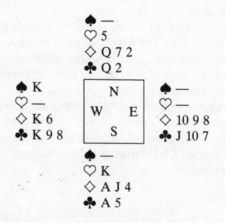

Sure enough, declarer now produced the ace and another diamond. West won with the king, his third trick, but had only clubs and spades left to play. The king of spades gives a ruff and discard while a club enables declarer to play this suit without loss. Either way the contract was now home and dry.

Aunt Agatha was, understandably, delighted with herself and made no effort to hide her emotions. On the other hand, it was clear that Issie felt he had been rather hard done by.

'Who would have thought that it was fatal for me to play even one top spade?' he moaned, although nobody seemed to be listening.

It is true that without Issie's assistance Aunt Agatha has not got the entries to eliminate spades and retain one trump in dummy for the end-game. Having seen the dummy, Issie did his best by switching to a trump at trick two, but the tempo was conceded and Aunt Agatha had her head in front all the way to the end-position.

In the other room Dottie and Percy were one down in 4 ♠ doubled after North found the killing lead of a trump.

THE LAST SAY

Aunt Agatha was a little surprised at the hand that went down on the table, obviously expecting more. I would like to have obliged, but one must remember that some of the niceties that automatically take place in a duet have to be forsaken once an opponent butts in. If you have a fit for partner's suit it is usually best to say so at once, rather than having to guess at some higher level.

As to Issie's lead, I really think a trump is quite attractive.*
With both minor suits held in check there is no necessity to cash
the spades at speed. Notice carefully Aunt Agatha's play of the
ace and another diamond, not the ace and another club. If West
has a third diamond, instead of a club, that is just too bad. The
contract will fail. But nothing is gained by playing the ace and
another club, because West can then concede a ruff and discard
with impunity.

Good play and good luck often seem to go together. If you
can manage the former, it is curious how often the latter
appears in a full supporting role.

*It would also be imperative if the North–South hands were
something like this:

♠ J 7
♡ K 4 2
♢ Q 7 4 2
♣ Q 10 5 2

```
      N
  W       E
      S
```

♠ 9 4 3 2
♡ A Q J 10 9 7 5
♢ A
♣ A

It was not long before Aunt Agatha was once again in the hot seat.

East-West game ♠ 8 6 4
Dealer East ♡ 7 6 5 4 2
 ◇ 6
 ♣ A 9 5 4

```
        N
    W       E
        S
```

 ♠ K Q J
 ♡ A K J 10 9 8
 ◇ 4
 ♣ Q 6 3

East passed, South opened 1 ♡ and West doubled. In what contract would you like to play? In the other room they settled for 3 ♡, which was just made. In our room this was the full auction:

S (A.A.)	W	N (F.N.)	E
—	—	—	No
1 ♡	Dble	3 ♡	4 ◇
4 ♡	No	No	No

Once more Aunt Agatha didn't seem over-impressed with my raise, but after the previous success she settled for a disapproving frown. West led the knave of diamonds, won by East's ace. East switched to the two of spades. West won this trick with the ace and returned the ten of spades. The outstanding trumps were drawn in one round, West holding the queen and East the three. How should declarer proceed?

Having cashed her spade winner, Aunt Agatha had a

straightforward problem: how should she avoid the loss of two club tricks? East had turned up with the ace of diamonds, and by inference must hold the queen, so it seemed likely that West held the king of clubs. But what about the knave and ten? If West held all three club honours, then a small club towards dummy was the right play, but if East held J x or 10 x a small club would be fatal. This was the complete deal:

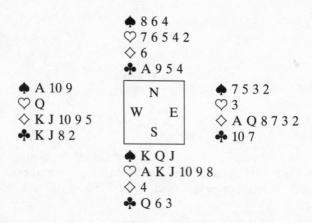

```
                    ♠ 8 6 4
                    ♡ 7 6 5 4 2
                    ◇ 6
                    ♣ A 9 5 4
  ♠ A 10 9          ┌─────────┐       ♠ 7 5 3 2
  ♡ Q              │    N    │       ♡ 3
  ◇ K J 10 9 5      │  W   E  │       ◇ A Q 8 7 3 2
  ♣ K J 8 2         │    S    │       ♣ 10 7
                    └─────────┘
                    ♠ K Q J
                    ♡ A K J 10 9 8
                    ◇ 4
                    ♣ Q 6 3
```

It didn't take Aunt Agatha long to make her mind up, and out flashed the queen of clubs. West covered, and so did dummy. East hovered for a moment before playing the seven but in any case there was no escape. A second club left East with the lead and West powerless to help. The resulting ruff and discard was Aunt Agatha's tenth trick. Of course, if East unblocks with the ten of clubs declarer only has to return to hand with a trump and lead a low club towards the nine.

'You were a bit thin for your double raise, weren't you?' enquired Aunt Agatha, almost graciously for once. I couldn't help wondering what she would have said had she misguessed the clubs. As it was, Aunt Agatha permitted herself a tiny smile when I replied, 'I would never have given it to you without the nine of clubs.'

THE LAST SAY

Despite Aunt Agatha's implied criticism, 3 ♡ is a fairly normal bid over a double. With a genuine raise to three of partner's suit one would use the conventional response of 2NT (otherwise a wasted bid); thus the direct raise to three is used for what one might term a stretch-barrage bid.

Aunt Agatha's play of the club suit was well reasoned, although perhaps rather lucky. It was fair to assume that West had the king of clubs and length in the suit, probably four, and it was more likely that East held one of the vital cards—the knave or the ten—than West held them both. For all that it was a close decision.

Aunt Agatha made short work of the next hand.

Love all   (F.N.)
Dealer South

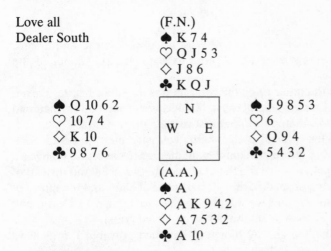

```
                    (F.N.)
                    ♠ K 7 4
                    ♡ Q J 5 3
                    ◇ J 8 6
                    ♣ K Q J
♠ Q 10 6 2                         ♠ J 9 8 5 3
♡ 10 7 4       N                   ♡ 6
◇ K 10      W     E                ◇ Q 9 4
♣ 9 8 7 6         S                ♣ 5 4 3 2
                    (A.A.)
                    ♠ A
                    ♡ A K 9 4 2
                    ◇ A 7 5 3 2
                    ♣ A 10
```

The bidding was brief: 1 ♡–4 ♡; 6 ♡. West led the nine of clubs. How should declarer plan the play?

Aunt Agatha began by cashing the four aces. The ace of

clubs, the ace of hearts, the ace of spades and the ace of diamonds—in that order. She then drew trumps, played off the king and queen of clubs and king of spades and ruffed a spade to arrive at the following position:

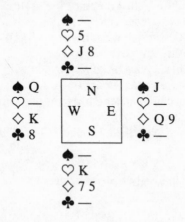

A diamond now forced West to concede a ruff and discard which enabled Aunt Agatha to claim the remainder of the tricks.

In the other room the contract was only four hearts. Eleven tricks were made because the declarer played a low diamond towards dummy without first cashing the ace.

'What a lot of useless cards you gave me!' observed Aunt Agatha, more to compliment her own expertise than as a complaint. 'Give me the king and another diamond instead of the king of spades, the queen, knave of clubs and the knave of diamonds, and we might have had to explain to Dottie and Percy how we came to miss a lay-down grand.'

'That's a ghastly thought,' I replied gravely. 'I'm glad we didn't have to face up to it.'

Aunt Agatha shot me a suspicious look, but I managed to keep a straight face with some difficulty and then turned the conversation back to our actual holdings.

'It was just as well I gave you the knave of diamonds,' I said, putting my finger on what was really the critical feature of the hand. However, it was clear from my aunt's almost contemptuous snort that she thought she would have made her contract with or without my diamond honour.

THE LAST SAY

With any small diamond instead of the ten, West could, and should, ditch his king of diamonds on the ace, thereby unblocking the suit. However, to give Aunt Agatha her due, it was because of the fear that West might unblock that she cashed the ace of diamonds early on. Cashing all the aces, one after the other, may have looked a bit like kitchen bridge, but it was all part of the general plan to camouflage the area in which the main attack was to be launched.

It is perhaps worth observing that from a defender's point of view it is always suspicious when the declarer cashes off a possibly unsupported ace in a high-level contract. More often than not the play is about to be projected to a position similar to that contrived by Aunt Agatha so the defender in the hot seat does well to unblock. An experienced declarer will cash his ace at the first opportune moment, hoping to mask his more sinister intentions. A lesser performer will complete his elimination programme and then cash his ace, giving the defence every opportunity to find an effective counter.

Suppose you are in a small slam and this is a side suit, with plenty of trumps in both hands and no outside loser:

$$7\ 5\ 4$$
$$K\ J \qquad\qquad Q\ 10\ 9$$
$$A\ 8\ 6\ 3\ 2$$

The sooner declarer cashes that ace the better his chance that

West will fail to unblock. Nevertheless, the king on the ace will usually be the right defence.

The points were certainly starting to flow Aunt Agatha's way as she fought our battle practically single-handed. On the following deal she engineered yet another big swing:

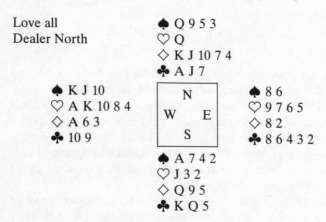

Love all
Dealer North

♠ Q 9 5 3
♡ Q
♢ K J 10 7 4
♣ A J 7

♠ K J 10
♡ A K 10 8 4
♢ A 6 3
♣ 10 9

♠ 8 6
♡ 9 7 6 5
♢ 8 2
♣ 8 6 4 3 2

♠ A 7 4 2
♡ J 3 2
♢ Q 9 5
♣ K Q 5

This was the bidding in Room 2 where Aunt Agatha sat West:

S	W (A.A.)	N	E (F.N.)
—	—	1 ♢	No
1 ♠	2 ♡	2 ♠	No
3 ♡	No	4 ♠	No
No	No		

In Room 1 South had also arrived in 4 ♠ and had no difficulty in making ten tricks. The losers were one heart, one spade and one diamond.

In Room 2 Aunt Agatha cashed a top heart and switched to the ten of clubs. Declarer won in hand and laid down the ace of spades. It was at this point that a strange thing happened—

Aunt Agatha dropped the king of spades on declarer's ace!

Recoiling from this apparent thunderbolt, South realized that he could not continue to draw trumps (assuming they were 4–1) until he had knocked out the ace of diamonds. So the queen of diamonds came next, and when that held the nine of diamonds followed. Aunt Agatha pounced on the second diamond and noting my peter duly gave me a ruff. Of course, Aunt Agatha still had to make a trump trick, so that was one down.

'Why didn't you just draw the trumps?' moaned North a little thoughtlessly.

'But I was sure . . .' began the declarer, 'well, that is to say when Agatha pulled out the wrong card it had me fooled completely. What a lucky mistake for them to make!'

Just as I was expecting Aunt Agatha to explode I suddenly realized that she was going to adopt an unfamiliar role. She was going to remain silent. Amazing! No doubt she enjoyed every moment of the confusion as she sat there like the cat that had just filched the Sunday joint. Apparently she didn't consider her opponents worthy of an explanation, since they had failed to recognize greatness even when it was right in front of their eyes.

THE LAST SAY

Aunt Agatha's play to the first round of trumps is in fact quite a well-known gambit. Although, superficially, it may appear crazy to throw away the master trump, the truth is that the actual cost is precisely nil. Suppose West plays the ten of spades on the first round, now South will surely continue the suit and it is clear that the defence can make no more than one trump trick. So the two plays are equal, trickwise. But the advantage of Aunt Agatha's choice is that it may persuade the declarer to pursue some other fatal or less rewarding line.

Luck was not with us on the next hand, and no amount of wriggling would have helped Aunt Agatha to extricate herself from the mire.

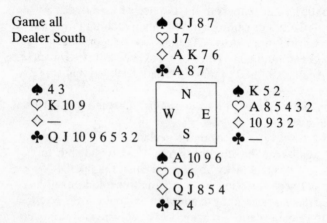

Game all   ♠ Q J 8 7
Dealer South   ♡ J 7
                    ◇ A K 7 6
                    ♣ A 8 7

♠ 4 3   ♠ K 5 2
♡ K 10 9   ♡ A 8 5 4 3 2
◇ —   ◇ 10 9 3 2
♣ Q J 10 9 6 5 3 2   ♣ —

                    ♠ A 10 9 6
                    ♡ Q 6
                    ◇ Q J 8 5 4
                    ♣ K 4

This was the bidding:

S	W	N	E
(A.A.)		(F.N.)	
1 ◇	2 ♣	3 ♣	No
3 ♠	No	4 ♠	No
No	No		

Of course, you can see that Aunt Agatha is going to have a rough ride because of the double void. And so it transpired. West led the queen of clubs which East ruffed. A low heart to the king was followed by the *two* of clubs for the second ruff. A well-disciplined East now switched to the ten of diamonds which West ruffed. The ace of hearts and a second diamond ruff completed the rout for a loss of 300.

Aunt Agatha was not particularly perturbed at the time. The ruffs were annoying, but presumably Dottie and Percy would inflict the same punishment on Issie so there could hardly be an adverse swing on the board, or so we thought. However, Dottie and Percy were not put to the test, as Issie did not play the hand in 4 ♠. The bidding was the same up to 3 ♣, but then Issie decided to conceal his spades and rebid 3NT which was passed out.

West led the queen of clubs, and since declarer needed spade tricks for his contract he won in dummy and immediately took the spade finesse. That resulted in +660 to North–South and a total loss to Aunt Agatha of 960 on the board. Just to rub it in, you'll observe that even a heart lead does not break the contract because the suit is blocked.

When Aunt Agatha heard what had happened in the other room she was livid.

'How can people play so badly and not only get away with it but profit handsomely into the bargain?' she enquired. The question was purely rhetorical, like most of Aunt Agatha's questions. The trouble about receiving a reply is that it stops, or at least hinders, the questioner from continuing the monologue, and that is something Aunt Agatha endeavours to avoid at all cost.

THE LAST SAY

I am not sure that it is necessarily the worst feature of bridge that bad contracts are sometimes blessed with everything that is righteous and honourable while good contracts occasionally get hacked to pieces. The fact that every so often the expert takes an ignominious tumble while the palooka emerges triumphant is a small facet of the game that will never fail to intrigue both the participants and the bridge media. Tempering this apparent injustice is the more pertinent fact that expert technique will always prevail in the long term. If it did so *all* the time much of the gloss would be removed from the most fascinating card game in the world, and some players I know would be even more unbearable than they are at present.

There was another adverse swing on the next hand.

Game all   ♠ A J 6
Dealer East   ♡ A Q 9 8
                ◇ 7 6 5
                ♣ K 7 3

```
        N
    W       E
        S
```

♠ K Q 8
♡ J 7 4
◇ A K Q 9 4 3
♣ 8

Both sides arrived in 6 ◇ by South. There was no opposition bidding and the lead was the two of spades. How would you plan the play?

This was the full hand:

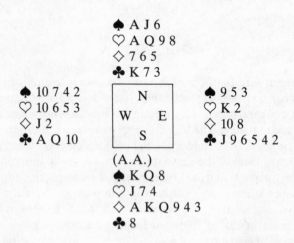

                   ♠ A J 6
                   ♡ A Q 9 8
                   ◇ 7 6 5
                   ♣ K 7 3

♠ 10 7 4 2   ♠ 9 5 3
♡ 10 6 5 3   ♡ K 2
◇ J 2   ◇ 10 8
♣ A Q 10   ♣ J 9 6 5 4 2

                   (A.A.)
                   ♠ K Q 8
                   ♡ J 7 4
                   ◇ A K Q 9 4 3
                   ♣ 8

Aunt Agatha won the spade lead in dummy with the ace, drew trumps and then played a club towards the king. West hopped up with the ace of clubs and eventually East had to make the king of hearts. That was +100 to the enemy.

When Dottie and Percy defended the hand the first three tricks were the same, but then declarer played a heart to dummy's queen and East's king. Rather naively East returned a spade and West, who was in any case subject to a successful heart finesse, had to surrender when the last trump was played in the following position:

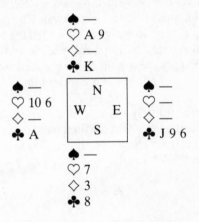

So that was another 1,370 to Issie's team, and a total swing of 18 imps.

Aunt Agatha had plenty to say about this loss, feeling that once again there had been a complete travesty of justice.

'That idiot,' she fumed, 'played the hand upside down and then profited because of an asinine mistake. Had there been any justice at all the ace of clubs would have been wrong and both heart honours right.'

THE LAST SAY

Although I have much sympathy for Aunt Agatha's *cri de cœur*, 'We wuz robbed', there is a little more to this problem than the straightforward odds. Clearly the best mathematical chance is to play for the ace of clubs to be right, and if it is for the king of hearts to be right as well. As a stand-by, should the ace of clubs be with East, declarer can fall back on the double heart finesse—the king and ten of hearts to be with West. However, taking the heart finesse before playing a club is not entirely crazy if East happens to be a weak player. The spade situation should not be difficult to interpret (West led the two, therefore South holds three spades. Furthermore, the suit must be solid otherwise why play the ace on the first round?) so that a club return from East stands out like a sore thumb.

The match was still very much in the balance as the last few boards were dealt, but it was the final hand of all that afforded Aunt Agatha a great chance to shine. This was the deal that positively breathed dynamite.

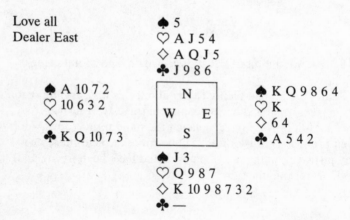

Love all   ♠ 5
Dealer East   ♡ A J 5 4
              ◇ A Q J 5
              ♣ J 9 8 6

♠ A 10 7 2   ♠ K Q 9 8 6 4
♡ 10 6 3 2   ♡ K
◇ —   ◇ 6 4
♣ K Q 10 7 3   ♣ A 5 4 2

              ♠ J 3
              ♡ Q 9 8 7
              ◇ K 10 9 8 7 3 2
              ♣ —

In the other room this was the bidding:

S	W	N	E
(Percy)	(Mildred)	(Dottie)	(Issie)
—	—	—	1 ♠
2 ♢	4 ♠	5 ♢	5 ♠
6 ♢	No	No	Dble
No	No	No	

Mildred cashed the ace of spades and switched to the king of clubs. Eventually Percy had to tackle the heart suit and lost a trick to East's king. One down. 100 points to Issie.

Issie was cock-a-hoop over the result.

'You notice, Mildred, we can't make six of anything,' he gloated. 'We must lose one heart and one club. Such a lucky result for us, because I'm sure Agatha won't stop short of slam.'

That was a fair assessment, in a limited sort of way, but it grossly underrated Aunt Agatha who is hardly an ideal subject for cold, clinical analysis.

Of course, Issie was partly right about the result in our room because Aunt Agatha (East) was indeed the declarer in 6 ♠ doubled. South had bid diamonds and had been strongly supported by his partner, who doubled the final contract.

South pondered over his lead for some time but couldn't think of anything better than the *two* of diamonds, an obvious McKenney requesting a club return.

Aunt Agatha liked what she saw and for once it seemed that my bidding, which in any case had been pretty pedestrian, met with approval. Evidently the full significance of the opening lead had not yet percolated through otherwise I might have been accused of overbidding again. However, it was not long before Aunt Agatha unearthed the grisly details. Having drawn trumps and ruffed her second diamond in dummy, she played the king of clubs—and the news was out. On the surface it seemed that declarer was faced with two inescapable losers, just as Issie had predicted. But Aunt Agatha does not accept defeat too readily and she found a line of play that Issie, in his superficial analysis, had overlooked. The ace of clubs was followed by three more rounds of spades to arrive at the following position. East to play, having won the first nine tricks:

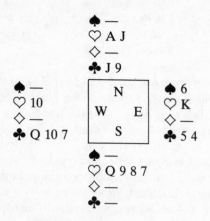

When Aunt Agatha played her last spade North was in trouble. In fact he parted with the knave of hearts, but then the king of hearts sealed his last bolt-hole. So that was 1,210 to Aunt Agatha, representing a swing of 15 imps on the board.

Of course, an original heart lead would have given Aunt Agatha no chance, and perhaps South should have found it. Issie claimed it was automatic, but I am inclined to the view that most thinking players in the South seat would have chosen the two of diamonds.

All Aunt Agatha claimed was that justice prevailed in the end!

THE LAST SAY

Going back to the first room, I wonder if you were completely happy with Percy's handling of the play in his contract of 6 ◇

doubled? Remember, Mildred (West) cashed the ace of spades and then switched to the king of clubs—presumably marking her with the queen as well. But it was East who opened the bidding and it is doubtful if he would have done so with only three honour cards, the ace of clubs and the king, queen of spades. So an alert South might have concluded that the king of hearts must be with East. Calling for the ace on the first round would have made some uninitiated eyebrows hit the ceiling, but it would have been quite a coup.

Without wishing to take anything away from Aunt Agatha, her slam was a little easier than Percy's. Having recovered from the initial shock of the clubs failing to break, there was only one way to succeed, and it was fifty pounds to a pinch of snuff that she would find it.

Rather grudgingly I had to admit that it had been an enthralling contest with many fascinating hands. At the final count Aunt Agatha emerged just in front. Perhaps her reply to an inquisitive fan who wanted to know how the match had gone sums it all up. '*I* won it—of course!'

Now where have I heard that before?